ASHES
OF THE
DIVINE

Daniel Lazaros Shahbaz Ali

ISBN
Paperback 979-8-89906-634-4
Hardcase 979-8-89961-596-2

CONTENTS

Chapter 1
THE INTRODUCTION

Payja was born in a small village and grew up in an ordinary, humble family. He didn't receive a basic education, not because he lacked the will, but because no one in his family had pursued education before him. Their priorities had always been centered around managing their agricultural land, tending to their cattle, and running the small businesses they owned in the village.

Despite these challenges, Payja was a young, handsome, and slender man. His family's livelihood came from a modest hand tractor wash and a small TV and radio repair shop.

Payja was a young, handsome, and slender man. His family's Payja usually woke up early in the morning—not out of devotion to prayer, responsibility for the cattle, or any business task, but because he had no other choice. In their joint family, when the elders woke at dawn, everyone else had to wake up too. The women would rise early to milk the cattle, while the men prepared the fire for the hookah, which they kept lit at the *dera* a communal space where villagers would gather to sit, chat, and share stories.

With their small house bustling with early-morning activity, there was no chance for Payja to sleep in, even if he wanted to. The bustling sound of the water pump filling up the water tank echoed through the house. His mother's loud voice came from the kitchen as she searched for a matchbox to light the stove.

Someone had forgotten to put the milk away properly, and during the night, the cat had drunk it—the same milk meant to be turned into yogurt.

Now, the morning quarrel began. His brother was arguing with his wife, scolding her for being careless about the milk. These sounds, the pump, the raised voices, and the petty arguments, were all part of Payja's daily life. In their home, these small chaos-filled moments weren't extraordinary; they were simply routine.

In their household, the grandfather was the ultimate authority, followed by the father. In families like theirs, authority was determined by age and experience. However, someone could gain more respect if they earned more than the other family members. Despite the hierarchy, it was common for anyone older to shout at someone younger, and in some cases, even administer a slap or two if they felt it was necessary to maintain order.

Meals were always eaten in the kitchen, near the fire stove. Small wooden stools were placed for everyone to sit on. In the mornings, they ate chapatis with milk or yogurt. Lassi, made from yogurt, was a staple drink and was believed to be a healthy start to the day. Everyone ate as many chapatis as they could until their stomachs were completely full.

The chapatis were made from wheat flour, and the wheat was grown in their own fields. On average, a family member could consume around forty kilos of wheat and drink about forty liters of milk per month. This simple yet abundant diet reflected life in the village, where the land itself was the greatest provider of food for the community.

Payja wasn't an active or driven person; his pace in life was slow and unhurried. He usually arrived at his repair shop well after the sun was high in the sky. Yet, every time he showed up, he was impeccably dressed, a cigarette often between his fingers. As the youngest of his brothers, he enjoyed a unique position in the family. Everyone cared for him, and he had certain privileges. If one of his older brothers lost their temper and tried to discipline him, there were always others ready to intervene on his behalf.

Payja's personality was peculiar compared to the rest of the family. While they followed more conventional paths, he dabbled in chemical experiments. He wasn't a scientist in the formal sense but more of a *sanyasi*. In local terms, a *sanyasi* referred to someone who wandered through forests, deserts, rivers, and mountains, collecting herbs to experiment with and create medicines. These medicines were often designed to address intimate issues, such as enhancing men's vitality or helping women who struggled with infertility.

Unlike most *sanyasis*, who lived solitary, wandering lives without families, Payja was different. He was a well-dressed figure in the village, always maintaining a sense of style and charm. He also had a wide circle of friends, many of whom were Ayurvedic healers and fellow *sanyasis*. Despite his unconventional character, his charisma and connections made him a prominent and somewhat mysterious figure in the community.

Payja's workshop doubled as a gathering spot for villagers seeking advice, remedies, or simply a bit of entertainment. One day, a villager arrived at the shop, clutching a bundle of dried herbs he'd collected from a nearby forest. "Payja," he said, "I heard these can help with joint pain. What do you think?"

Payja inspected the herbs with a practiced eye, rolling a sprig between his fingers and sniffing it. "Not bad," he said, exhaling a puff of smoke, "but it's missing something. Come back tomorrow, and I'll show you what to mix it with."

That night, Payja worked late. Under the dim light of a lantern, he grounds the herbs with powders and oils he'd obtained from his Ayurvedic healer friends. By morning, he had created a paste that he confidently handed to the villager.

"Rub this on the joints twice a day," he instructed. "But don't expect miracles. It'll ease the pain, not erase it."

Word of his remedy spread quickly, and soon others came seeking his advice. Though he wasn't formally trained, Payja's instincts and experimentation earned him a reputation as someone who could bridge tradition and innovation.

Unlike most *Sanyasi's*, who lived solitary, wandering lives without families, Payja was different. He was a well-dressed figure in the village, always maintaining a sense of style and charm. He also had a wide circle of friends, many of whom were Ayurvedic healers and fellow *sanyasis*. Despite his unconventional character, his charisma and connections made him a prominent and somewhat mysterious figure in the community.

Payja's circle of friends was as colorful and intriguing as he was. There was Rana, Baba, Daniel, Kala, Rasha, and Mian—a mix of personalities who would come and go throughout the day, turning his repair shop into a lively hub of conversation and activity. Payja made it a point to always offer tea or cigarettes to his guests, sometimes even lunch or cold drinks. It was part of his charm, but it did not sit well with his brothers.

His brothers often complained about his spending habits. "Why waste so much money on tea and cigarettes for your friends?" they would grumble. "It's not like they're paying you back!"

But Payja would only smile in response. "You think I'm just wasting my time as a *sanyasi*?" he would reply. "Let me tell you, these friends of mine are not just here for tea. They are helping me in ways you cannot see—finding herbs, gathering information, and guiding me closer to my goal."

Among his brothers, Tara—the one who was effectively in charge of the family—was the most patient with him. Tara would often listen attentively to Payja's words, his stern expression softening as he asked, "And when will this big plan of yours happen, Payja?"

Payja's answer was always the same. "It is just a little longer, brother. A little more, and we'll be done. Don't worry; there will be money for everyone!"

Though Tara didn't always understand Payja's methods, his words carried a quiet conviction that was hard to dismiss. Each time Payja spoke, Tara's eyes would light up with hope, a rare smile crossing his face. Payja's unwavering confidence had a way of disarming even the most skeptical minds, and Tara, despite his responsibilities, found himself believing in his younger brother's promises.

Most of Payja's experiments revolved around the creation of *kushtas*. A *kushta* is a type of herbal medicine, often made from metals like iron or nickel, or even from dangerous poisons. The process of making *kushtas* is extremely complex and delicate. If something goes wrong, the resulting product could lead to fatal poisoning or severe side effects for the patient.

Metals like iron (*loha*) or tin (*qalai*) are considered relatively safe for *kushta* preparation. These are carefully processed to transform their properties, making them suitable for healing. *Kushta* refers to a medicine that has been burned or calcined, a process believed to enhance its potency and efficacy. This ancient technique has been used in traditional medicine for centuries to treat various ailments.

However, *sanyasis* like Payja often worked with far more dangerous substances. They used toxic minerals and poisons, aiming to neutralize their harmful properties and harness their potential benefits. Substances that would ordinarily be fatal if ingested or even tasted were transformed through intricate procedures into medicines thought to treat diseases that no ordinary remedy could cure.

This risky craft required not only knowledge but also precision and courage. A single mistake could be catastrophic, but when done correctly, *kushtas* were considered miraculous, capable of curing illnesses that seemed otherwise hopeless.

Payja's experiments reflected both the allure and the danger of this ancient practice. While many in the village admired his skill and curiosity, others whispered about the risks he took not just for himself but for those who trusted his remedies.

One day, Payja was engrossed in one of his most dangerous experiments. He was working with copper sulfate, a potent poison that required extreme caution. The process involved heating the substance over an open flame, carefully controlling the temperature to avoid any mishaps. But something went terribly wrong.

The fire flared unexpectedly, sending toxic smoke billowing through the small room. Payja, caught off guard, inhaled the fumes before he could escape. The acrid smoke burned his lungs, and he collapsed, coughing violently. His family rushed him to the hospital, where doctors worked to save him.

His condition was severe; the damage to his lungs resembled the effects of advanced tuberculosis. For weeks, he struggled to breathe, confined to a hospital bed, his usually bright and optimistic demeanor dimmed by the gravity of his injuries. But somehow, against the odds, Payja survived.

When he finally returned home, his family pleaded with him to abandon his experiments. "Payja, look what this has done to you!" Tara said, his voice filled with a mix of anger and concern. "Do you want to kill yourself? Enough with these poisons!"

But Payja, true to his nature, simply smiled. "Tara, you don't understand," he replied, his voice raspier now but no less resolute. "This is not just about experiments. It is about finding something extraordinary. I cannot stop now."

Daniel, one of Payja's closest friends, visited him daily. A farmer by trademark, Daniel also looked after his cattle cows and buffaloes which kept him busy for much of the day. Unlike many in the village, Daniel was educated and known for his quick wit and smart demeanor.

In the evenings, Payja and Daniel often gathered at Rana's place, a familiar spot where friends came together to unwind. A few others always joined them, turning the gathering into a lively affair. They spent their time playing cards, sharing jokes, and enjoying the simple pleasures of life. Tea was a staple at these gatherings, and occasionally, they would indulge in a meal if someone brought something to share.

These evenings were a highlight for Payja, offering him a chance to momentarily set aside his experiments and enjoy the camaraderie of his friends. For Daniel, it was a welcome break from the routine of farm life, a chance to recharge his mind and enjoy the company of like-minded souls.

"She came today I saw her," Rana said casually, his eyes on the cards in his hand. "When you took her upstairs to the repair shop... So, did you damage her, or fix something?"

"Shut up! Why are you spying on me?" Payja snapped, his tone sharp with irritation.

Rana smirked, unfazed. "Last time, I heard her eyes nearly popped out when you... you know..." He trailed off, bursting into laughter.

Daniel could not resist joining in. "That's because Payja has a huge key, and the lock is tiny!" he said, barely able to contain his laughter.

"It's true!" Baba chimed in, grinning as he entered the conversation. "That's why our Payja is so famous because of his big key."

"And that's why he has to buy so much mustard oil every week!" Rana added, doubling over with laughter.

"Enough!" Payja said, shaking his head with a smile as their teasing reached its peak. "You are all just small-key men, jealous because you've got no keys to open any locks. But me? I don't just open locks, I break them when my key enters. That's why you can't stand me!"

The room erupted in laughter again, the air was thick with cigarette smoke and the warmth of playful camaraderie. Even Payja couldn't help but grin at their relentless humor, knowing that behind all the teasing was a bond that tied them together like brothers.

Payja had a secret girlfriend from a nearby village, a woman known for her striking beauty but also for her controversial reputation. Her name was Rani. She came from a family of two sisters, both equally beautiful and often the subject of gossip. In their society, where a woman's behavior was heavily scrutinized, the sisters' easygoing and independent nature made them targets for judgment.

Unlike most women in the village, they were frequently seen active, unbothered by the whispers that followed them. They talked openly with men, which was enough for people to label them as women of loose character. Despite the rumors, the sisters were not involved in anything transactional. Their relationships with their boyfriends, including Payja, were based on genuine connection rather than money. Yet, the mere fact that they had boyfriends was enough to make them notorious in the eyes of the village men.

One sister often spent time with Payja, while the other was known to be with someone else. Their unconventional relationships defied societal norms, making them both admired and condemned. For Payja, however, his connection to his girlfriend wasn't about what others thought. She was vibrant, bold, and unlike anyone else he knew a stark contrast to the rigid expectations of their community.

This dynamic wasn't unique to their village. Even in many other parts of the world, the idea of women having male friends or maintaining relationships outside of marriage was considered taboo, often resulting in harsh judgments. It was a stark reminder of how deeply rooted cultural norms could shape perceptions of morality and character, especially for women.

"When are you doing your next experiment?" Baba asked, his curiosity was evident.

"Tomorrow," Payja replied, leaning forward. "We'll go to the bank of the river. There's an herb called *hazardani*. I've heard it only grows by the riverbank. And if I could also find *mushk booti*, the herb found in the mountains of the Himalayas, I'm certain we'd succeed."

"The mountains are so far away from here," Baba said, his tone skeptical.

"I know," Payja acknowledged, "but I have a friend in Kashmir—you know Qari? He's been inviting me to visit for ages. If I go, I'll search for *mushk booti* there."

Daniel, who had been silently listening, suddenly interjected, shaking his head. "Oh, stop this nonsense! Did you even watch the news recently? Science has reached the moon! Men have walked on the moon, and you're still talking about herbs. No one can turn copper into gold or nickel into silver. Gold has a completely different atomic structure; its protons aren't the same as copper's. Same for silver and nickel. It's impossible!"

Baba scoffed. "What do you know about science, Daniel?" he countered. "In everything, there is the essence of *Maha Atma*. He can turn anything into anything. He is in you, in me, in the birds, the trees, and the herbs. How do you think people find gold in the mines? He made it! He turned sand into gold, into metals, into diamonds. Coal and diamonds are found in the same place, yet they are so different. It is only a matter of time before our God, *Maha Atma,* is pleased with us and blesses us with the technique to turn copper into gold."

Daniel rolled his eyes. "That's a nice story, Baba, but science has already shown us how gold is formed and where to find it. It's not magic. All metals have unique atomic structures. You can't just change one into another."

"Oh, stop it, you! big scientist," Rana cut in, smirking at Daniel. "You can argue all you want, but tomorrow you're going with Payja to the riverbank to find this *hazardani* herb. Take Kala with you too."

"Fine," Daniel said, throwing up his hands in mock surrender. "We'll go after breakfast, first thing in the morning."

"Dear friend, focus on your game instead of your science lectures. Right now, we are losing," Rana said to Daniel, trying to hide his smirk.

"Oh, no, wait, Rana. I have got something up my sleeve—we are not losing yet," Daniel replied, a confident smile spreading across his face as he adjusted his cards.

"That's it!" Daniel shouted triumphantly, throwing his last card onto the table with a loud "Hurrah!"

Rana burst into laughter. "You see, Payja? You have lost again!" he said, leaning back and enjoying the moment.

Payja frowned, turning to Baba with a look of mock frustration. "If you didn't have the ace, then why were you smiling?" he asked, clearly annoyed.

"I thought you had the ace," Baba replied sheepishly. "All I had was a queen."

"You don't watch my moves properly," Payja argued, shaking his head. "If I had the ace, why would I hold onto it until the end?"

Baba shrugged. "No problem. Next time, we will win," he said, patting Payja on the back.

"Yeah, sure," Rana teased, laughing again. "Next time, you'll win—and then your son will wake you up for the morning prayer!"

The room filled with laughter once more, their banter bouncing off the walls like echoes of their carefree camaraderie. Despite the defeat, Payja could not help but crack a small smile, already looking forward to the next round.

Chapter 2

FINDING THE HAZARDANI

The morning sun was just beginning to rise, painting the sky in hues of pink and orange, when Payja, Daniel, and Kala set off for the riverbank. Their destination wasn't far, but the journey felt significant, a mission steeped in both tradition and mystery.

"Do you think we'll really find it today? Daniel asked, adjusting the bag slang over his shoulder. It contained a few essentials: a small knife, some jars, and a bottle of water.

Payja, ever optimistic, exhaled a puff of cigarette smoke and smirked. "I don't think, Daniel, I know. *Hazardani* grows by the water, and the river has always provided for those who seek."

Kala, usually the quietest of the group, chuckled softly. "Let's hope it doesn't provide us with snakes instead," he said, scanning the tall grasses ahead.

The path to the riverbank was narrow and uneven, flanked by wild bushes and scattered stones. The cool morning air carried the earthy scent of damp soil and the faint murmur of the river in the distance. Their conversation drifted between lighthearted jokes and serious planning; each man buoyed by the shared excitement of discovery.

By the time they reached the river, the sun was fully up, casting a golden glow over the flowing water. Payja knelt by the edge, his eyes scanning the plants growing along the muddy banks. "This is the spot," he declared, pulling out a small spade.

"Let's just hope it doesn't take all day," Daniel muttered, though he couldn't hide the spark of curiosity in his voice.

"Patience, my friend," Payja replied with a grin. "If this herb is as powerful as they say, it's worth every minute we spend looking for it."

As they began their search, the sound of the river and the rustle of leaves created a peaceful rhythm. Yet beneath the surface of their calm banter was a shared understanding: this was no ordinary herb. Finding *hazardani* could change everything, not just for Payja, but for all of them.

Weary and disoriented from their long search for Hazardani, they finally stopped to rest near the riverbank. The sun was dipping low, casting a golden shimmer on the flowing water. Payja reached into his coat pocket and pulled out a crumpled cigarette. With quiet focus, he began to peel it open, carefully emptying the tobacco into his palm. From another pocket, he retrieved a small piece of black resin—sticky and pungent. Holding it to the flame of a match, he warmed it until it softened, then blended it with the tobacco and refilled the cigarette. He did this patiently, rolling four of them with steady fingers.

Daniel watched the entire ritual, wide-eyed with curiosity. "What is that?" he finally asked, unable to hold back.

Payja grinned. "This," he said, holding up the cigarette like a sacred object, "is the drug of saints. When we smoke it, our minds double in speed, twice as sharp, twice as alive. Sun or snow, rain or heat, nothing bothers us after this."

He lit the first cigarette, took a slow drag, and passed the rest around. Baba and Daniel joined in, hesitant at first but soon drawn in by the smoothness of the smoke. It was hashish, its taste, lighter than tobacco, soft and mellow as it entered the lungs. The scent was earthy, unfamiliar, but soothing. When they exhaled, it felt as though even their breath had grown calm.

Suddenly, Daniel spoke. "My lungs feel tight… like they're shrinking. And my eyes, I can't even open them fully!"

Payja chuckled. "Wait a little. The real magic starts soon," he said, eyes sparkling.

Baba handed Daniel a small mirror he carried in his pocket. "Here. Look at your eyes," he said. "They're beautiful now."

Daniel took the mirror and stared at his reflection. His eyes glistened with moisture, and a soft, silly smile curved his lips. "God… I look amazing," he whispered, half-laughing.

They finished smoking all four hashish-laced cigarettes, the world around them beginning to melt into a slow, golden haze. Then they unpacked the food they had brought from the village and ate hungrily. But no matter how much they ate; the hunger didn't fade. They wandered into nearby fields, plucking fresh vegetables and watermelons. The sweet juice of the fruit only deepened the high, making their hearts race and laughter burst freely from their chests.

They had entirely forgotten why they'd come. Hazardani, the treasure, the mission, gone from memory like a dream fading at dawn. Instead, they wandered the fields like wild deer, light on their feet, weightless and free.

"Life is beautiful," someone said, though it wasn't clear who.

And truly, it was.

All it takes is a shift in perspective. Just one moment and everything changes.

They had been restless just moments ago, desperately searching for the sacred herb—Hazardani. Wandering in circles, unsure where to look next, frustration clung to them like dust. The weight of their quest was growing heavier with every step. But then… they paused. They sat by the riverbank, lit those strange hand-rolled cigarettes, and something shifted — drastically.

Was it just the effect of the drug?

Yes, perhaps. But Daniel, caught in the quiet storm of his thoughts, wondered — how many drugs does the human body already carry within?

How many chemicals do we create every day without even realizing it?

Our anger. Our joy. The warmth of a smile, or the sharp edge of sorrow. The way we react, love, fight, forgive, all of it, Daniel thought, stems from minuscule chemical dances inside our flesh. How strange that such small things decide so much of who we are.

While the others burst out laughing over nonsense and silly jokes, Daniel drifted deeper into thought. His mind had begun moving like a philosopher's, quiet, curious, questioning everything.

Why is it that we, as human beings, often fail to grasp the smallest truths?

The kind that can shift an entire world?

If just a pinch of hashish or a few drops of alcohol can turn an ordinary person into someone else entirely… then why can't we trigger such transformations ourselves? Without the help of anything external.

Is it possible?

"I think it is," Daniel whispered to himself.

He often spoke to himself this way. Not out of madness, but out of intimacy. He thought deeply, and when answers felt far, he would ask himself for guidance. In truth, *he* was his Favorite person to talk to. The one who always listened. The one who always understood.

"I've read about so many great minds," Daniel whispered softly to himself, "and what made them great wasn't just their philosophies, it was how they turned their thoughts into experiments. They didn't just think; they lived what they believed."

There was a faint smile on his lips as he noticed how much he liked whispering to himself. It felt honest. Private. Like speaking directly to the soul.

"And they weren't drug addicts, by the way," he added with a grin, amused at his own commentary.

Most of those philosophers, he thought, were deeply religious, or at least connected to some kind of spiritual belief. In ancient times, religion was the spine of society. It shaped laws, thoughts, behavior. When religion dominated the world, people either found comfort in it... or pressure. Some, perhaps many, felt suffocated. And it was under that pressure that certain minds rose—not necessarily to rebel, but to evolve. To question. To carve out freedom in a world that insisted on chains.

Daniel imagined those thinkers, those saints, scholars, and sages, who worked not to destroy religion, but to transcend it. They studied, they wrote, they explored. Through knowledge, discipline, and discovery, they earned a place so unique that even religion couldn't touch them. Their intelligence became their shield, their wisdom a sanctuary.

"Yes, there are many ways to look at it," Daniel murmured. "But now... now it feels different."

He looked around at the fields, the sky above beginning to darken with the coming evening. "We're not progressing like we once did," he thought. "There are fewer new philosophies, fewer inventions that shift the world. And we aren't even creating new religions anymore."

Maybe humanity had had enough of religion. Maybe we've learned too much, uncovered too many truths. Maybe the old stories of creation, once held sacred, now feel like ancient myths, no longer needed in a world of science and technology.

But even then, we rarely dare to speak against them. The weight of tradition still lingers.

"Deep inside," Daniel whispered, "we know those stories are false. But we don't have the courage to admit it aloud."

He paused. A breeze passed over him like a sigh from the earth.

And yet, he thought, *even if we don't speak it… we know. In our consciousness, in that silent part of the mind where truth sits patiently, we know.*

"Now I understand the truth of life," Daniel whispered to himself, his voice almost lost in the breeze.

"Yes... we human beings *can* create it. All of it—the transformation, change, elevation. We don't need anything external. Not drugs, not distractions. It's all already within us."

The thought settled over him like warm sunlight on skin.

"It's possible... yes. It really is," he murmured, eyes fixed on the horizon, though his vision was turned inward.

"But I must learn *how,*" Daniel said softly. There was no urgency in his tone, only quiet determination.

"I'll begin from now… I'll try to understand. How to be what I want to be, no matter what the situation. How to stay happy, even when the world gives me no reason to smile. How to become whatever I need to be, without waiting for the world to change."

The others were still laughing nearby, lost in their heights, but Daniel was somewhere else entirely now.

Not intoxicated, *awakening.*

A thought echoed through his mind like a vow:

I can be the architect of my own being.

And for the first time, the search for Hazardani no longer felt like a chase for a herb.

It was a metaphor.

The real treasure… was this moment of clarity.

As they neared the village, the golden haze of sunset touched the rooftops, and familiar voices drifted through the air. A group of old friends passed by on their way to the mosque for evening prayer. Without hesitation, Payja, Kalu, and Baba followed them inside, still high, their eyes heavy-lidded, their minds floating somewhere between worlds.

Daniel, however, remained outside, sitting quietly near the steps, curious to observe. He watched them enter the mosque with the same devotion they carried even when sober. For them, prayer was sacred, no matter what the state of their bodies. Drunk, high, or broken, they never skipped it. It wasn't about rules. It was about rhythm.

Inside, the imam began reciting verses from the Qur'an in a calm, melodic voice that echoed through the quiet hall. At first, everything seemed normal. The men stood in rows, heads bowed, moving in sync. But then Payja, standing in the second row, let out a soft chuckle. It began deep in his chest, like a tickle he couldn't control.

Kala heard it and started laughing too.

Then Baba joined in.

And like a spark in dry grass, laughter spread across the quiet hall, rippling uncontrollably.

Daniel, watching from behind the curtain of the doorway, couldn't help himself either. His shoulders shook as he tried not to burst out loud. The entire moment was surreal. The sacred silence of prayer was broken by uncontrollable, innocent laughter.

The imam paused, visibly confused. He ended the prayer and turned toward them with a mix of concern and disbelief.

"Please," he said, trying to remain calm, "let's stop laughing. Let's try again, with focus."

Everyone nodded solemnly. They lined up again, trying their best to suppress the laughter building in their chests like steam under pressure.

But as soon as the imam began reciting again, Payja let out another laugh, this time louder, like a child trying to be quiet but failing miserably. And that was it. They collapsed again into laughter. It didn't matter that they were in a mosque. It didn't even register. They were no longer fully present in this world.

The imam, baffled, had no idea what was happening. It never crossed his mind that someone under the influence of hashish would enter a mosque for prayer. But to Payja, Kala, and Baba, it made perfect sense.

Prayer is prayer, Payja would say, *no matter what state we're in. It's our duty. It's our love. Our personal mess with God is ours alone.*

Finally, the imam gave up. "Please," he sighed, "perform your prayer however you wish. I'll do mine separately."

He turned away, quietly continuing his own practice, leaving the others to theirs.

Outside, the friends emerged into the cooling night, their laughter slowly fading into contented smiles.

"Well," said Payja, stretching his arms, "we came. We stood. We tried. God saw us in the mosque, that's enough. He knows what's in the heart. I think our prayers are accepted anyway."

Everyone nodded, half serious, half amused. With that, they wandered off into the village streets, still wrapped in the strange peace of prayer, laughter, and smoke.

The next morning, reality began to creep back in, slowly but surely. The laughter of yesterday still echoed faintly in their minds, but with it came a heavy realization.

"What the hell were we even doing in the mosque?" said Kala, breaking the silence as they all gathered at Rana's place, sipping hot tea.

"It was a miracle no elder was there," muttered Baba, scratching his head. "Had someone respectable seen us, we'd be done for."

"Thank God the imam was our friend," said Payja. "Anyone else would've dragged us out by our collars. But he just left us alone."

Rana looked at them all in disbelief, especially Payja. "You idiots actually went to the mosque *high*?"

They shrugged.

"Yesterday, we wandered all day but didn't even find a trace of Hazardani," Payja said, sipping his tea.

"That's because I wasn't looking for Hazardani," Baba replied with a grin. "I just came to smoke hashish."

"Oh, and I was the only one smoking?" Payja raised an eyebrow.

"No, no," Baba chuckled. "But you were the one who brought the hash, rolled it into cigarettes, and handed it out. What were we supposed to do, refuse your hospitality?"

He glanced at Daniel. "Even Daniel had a puff. And man… he looked divine when he was high. His eyes were sparkling. Like a mystic or something."

"*What the hell!*" Rana snapped, his eyes narrowing at Payja. "Why did you give hash to Daniel? He's a simple guy. A good guy. Don't spoil him like you've spoiled yourselves!"

Payja leaned back and crossed his arms. "He could've said no if he was that good. But he didn't. He took it, smoked it, and smiled like the rest of us. So… he's one of us now."

Daniel looked up, calm and composed.

"Whether I'm like you or not doesn't matter," he said gently. "Yesterday, yes, we were all the same. But from today, don't offer me hash again."

"Oh?" said Payja, amused. "Why's that?"

Daniel smiled faintly. "Because I learned something. I don't need it. I can feel like that without smoking anything. I understood that it's possible to act, to feel, to *become*… just by choosing to."

Baba laughed. "Aha! You *actor*! Go on then, show us. Be that version of yourself again. No hash. Just you."

Daniel closed his eyes. Silence fell. He took a breath, deep and steady, and let his mind slip into the memory of the previous day. The feeling of weightlessness, of openness, of glowing eyes and soft speech, he reached into that space again, not through smoke but through thought.

Then he opened his eyes.

They sparkled.

His posture relaxed, his smile gentle and slow.

"You see me now," Daniel said softly. "I'm the same as yesterday."

Everyone stared, stunned. Even Baba was speechless.

"How the hell do you do that?" he asked finally. "You're a magician. Or you really are a damn good actor. You should join a theatre group."

Daniel laughed, not in mockery, but with peace.

"Or maybe," he said, "we've forgotten how powerful the mind really is."

"Alright, listen up," said Payja, standing tall with his teacup in hand. "Today, after lunch, we'll head to the far side of the river. And this time no hashish, no distractions. We won't return until we find Hazardani. Agreed?"

Everyone nodded in unison.

"Yes. Good idea," said Daniel, his voice calm but determined.

After lunch, Daniel met the others on the dusty road that led toward the riverbank. The sun hung high above them, and a light breeze stirred the wild grass. Their steps felt lighter today perhaps from purpose, perhaps from hope.

They crossed the river carefully, using a narrow strip of stone and wood that lay like a forgotten bridge. On the other hand, the world opened wide, lush and untouched, the kind of green that only lives far away from noise.

They began scanning the earth, moving slowly through patches of wild herbs and tangled undergrowth, their eyes searching for the sign they had memorized.

They hadn't walked far when Baba suddenly called out, excitement rising in his voice.

"Payja! Come here, quick! Look at this could it be?"

Payja jogged over, heart thumping in his chest. He crouched beside Baba and examined the plant closely. A slow smile spread across his face.

"Yes," he whispered. "This is it. This is Hazardani."

The herb was small, delicate, its leaves tiny like a mouse's ears, hugging the ground like it didn't want to be seen. But it was everywhere. Spread across the field like nature's secret, waiting only for those who knew how to look.

One by one, they fell to their knees, collecting it with care, filling their bags, their hands trembling with gratitude. For them, this wasn't just a plant, it was a treasure. A symbol of hope. A doorway to a future they believed in.

"Thank you, Mother Earth," whispered Payja, his voice full of reverence.

As they stood there, overwhelmed with joy, someone shouted with wild delight, "Soon we'll be able to make our *own* gold!"

Their laughter and cries echoed into the open sky, far from the village, where no one could hear them. It was a moment of pure, unfiltered freedom.

Their faces lit up, not with the glow of intoxication, but with the fire of discovery. Like a dying man suddenly flooded with adrenaline. Like a lover spotting his beloved at the end of a long wait.

They were alive.

They had found it.

And with full hearts, they began their walk back to the village, their steps now guided by something greater than hope.

Chapter 3

RANI

Rani lived in a quiet village not far from the one where Payja and Daniel resided. Her life, like many in that part of the world, was shaped by silence, customs, and the weight of unwritten rules. Her father had died when she was still a child, leaving her mother to raise her alone.

In that society, widowhood didn't always mean ruin, at least not publicly. Cultural and religious traditions encouraged support for widows, offering them food, shelter, and a place within the village. Most families had homes passed down through generations, and cows in their courtyards that provided milk, the very foundation of their daily meals. Life was simple, structured, but not without shadows.

Because beneath that structure, another reality pulsed. A widow might be offered food and shelter by the village, yes, but safety was another matter. Without a man in the house, some men saw it as an invitation. And in every society, there are always a few who feed on vulnerability.

To survive, many widows quietly aligned themselves with the most dangerous man they could find, the kind others feared to even look in the eye. Not out of love, not always out of choice, but out of necessity. Because in such places, protection was a currency, and fear was its sharpest edge.

Rani's mother, too, had a protector. Everyone in the village knew about her secret relationship, but no one dared to confront her. Why? Because the man she slept with was feared. And in this world, being feared was often more powerful than being respected.

Rani grew up watching this truth unfold, and she learned early: *Choose your man wisely, not for his kindness, but for his power.*

She chose Payja.

Payja wasn't the gentlest soul, but he was strong and more importantly, he had many brothers, all of them known for their temper and brute force. Together, they were untouchable. People spoke about Rani and Payja, how she visited him in broad daylight, how they didn't even bother hiding their intimacy. Everyone knew. But no one said a word. No one dared.

In a way, Rani had inherited her mother's survival instinct. And she'd made the same choice as her mother once did, strength over love, protection over judgment.

Because in this society, morality often bends to power.

Even religion looks the other way when fear walks into the room.

Criminals are tolerated, even admired, so long as they remain untouchable.

And justice rarely bothers those who hold the louder voice or the stronger hand.

Fear is a beautiful weapon, it can guard, or it can wound.

And the truth about fear is this: if you don't wield it, someone else will.

And even when you do... one day, someone stronger will come, holding that same weapon, and point it back at you.

Rani had always known one thing with certainty, so long as her name was tied to Payja, no man in the village, or beyond, would dare disturb her. She didn't need Payja to fight for her. His reputation alone was enough. Just the mention of their closeness kept unwanted eyes and unspoken threats at bay.

Her mother, Fatima, now in her fifties, was still striking, her features carried a kind of quiet strength, and her beauty had endured through hardship. She had raised Rani and her sister alone, and though life had tested her in many ways, she had never let the weight of widowhood break her.

One evening, as Rani was oiling her hair, Fatima sat down beside her with a familiar seriousness in her voice.

"I've told you before, haven't I? Payja isn't going to marry you," Fatima said gently but firmly. "I've found one of our relatives for you. He's financially stable. A decent man."

"I know," Rani replied, her voice calm. "But Mama… what do you think I'll do with that man, once I marry him, when my heart already belongs to Payja?"

Fatima sighed, brushing her daughter's hair with slow strokes. "I understand, my child. But you know he's already married. He has children. It's not right to break a home."

"But I'm not trying to ruin anything," Rani whispered. "I just love him. It's not only about protection anymore. It's… real."

Fatima stopped brushing for a moment. "I know, sweetheart. But we, as women, know what it feels like to be left alone. To be widowed or divorced. It's misery in this world. We don't want to become the reason another woman suffers the same fate."

"Then what should I do with my love?" Rani asked, her voice trembling.

"Nothing," Fatima said. "Keep loving him, like you do now. What's wrong with that? Boundaries, culture, religion, these things were not made for people like us. We do what we must to survive, to stay safe. You'll marry this man I've found, and you'll live a secure life. Meanwhile, your heart can stay with Payja. You'll still be able to see him, no one will stop you. After all, your friends are in his village. No one will question your visits."

Rani lowered her eyes, unsure.

Fatima continued, her voice is softer now. "You know as well as I do, love doesn't feed you. Payja… he's chasing some wild dream. He has no income. He's a *sanyasi* now, a man with no roots, no real path."

"But he promised me, Mama," Rani said, almost like a child. "He said the first time he makes gold; he'll make jewelry for me. For me, first."

Fatima chuckled lightly. "Then wait for that day. When he makes gold, you can leave this man and go to Payja. No one will stop you. But until then, you need to settle down. If you don't marry now, your younger sister won't find a suitable match either."

Fatima leaned in closer. "And listen this man, he's simple. Almost too simple, maybe even a bit foolish," she said with a laugh. "But he likes you. He told me he finds your eyes beautiful. He loves your hair. And Rani… he'll take care of you. No restrictions. A good house. A steady life."

Rani didn't respond immediately. Her heart was torn. She loved Payja, his fire, his madness, his wild dreams. But she loved her mother too. And more than anything, she trusted her.

So, with a quiet nod, Rani accepted her mother's decision.

She agreed to marry the man she had never met.

The next day, Rani came to visit Payja. Daniel happened to be sitting with him at his shop when she arrived, her younger sister Sonu walking by her side.

As soon as the sisters stepped in, Daniel's heart gave a jolt. His face lit up, though he tried not to show it. There was something untamed, almost elemental, about their beauty, like wildflowers growing free beyond the reach of any garden wall.

Payja greeted Rani with a kiss on the cheek, casual and bold. Then he turned to Daniel and grinned, "You both sit here and talk. We have some business upstairs."

Before Daniel could respond, Payja and Rani disappeared into the upper room, leaving him alone with Sonu.

But they weren't truly alone. There was another presence in that small room, a shadow without form, an ancient whisper in the blood. The Devil. Or at least, the idea of him.

Not the horned monster from fables, but something far more subtle: the invisible force that stirs the heart, that nudges flesh toward flesh, and labels the most sacred acts of human closeness as *sin*.

Daniel sat still, aware of Sonu's quiet breath beside him, the soft rustle of her dress, the scent of warm skin and sunlight in her hair.

And a thought stirred in him, soft but relentless.

Why is this a sin?

Why, in so many societies, are the holiest acts of love considered crimes? Why must two adults, aware of their bodies, their choices, their consequences, hide their tenderness in shame?

If love is God, Daniel wondered, *why does it feel like we must hide God from the world?*

He had never understood it. Never accepted it. Why does making love, with honesty and care, provoke such judgment? Why must it be whispered, forbidden, wrapped in guilt?

Perhaps the world had it backwards. Perhaps everything was reversed.

What if the God we worship is actually the Devil? And the Devil we fear is actually God?

What if every truth we've been taught is merely a reflection, flipped, distorted, misunderstood?

Of course we see things the opposite way, Daniel thought.

We always have.

Daniel and Sonu sat in silence, their eyes locked in a gaze that held everything and nothing at once. For Sonu, Daniel was just another man, like many before, looking at her with that familiar mix of longing and hesitation. She'd seen it all before. The curiosity, hunger, the fear of rejection hidden behind awkward smiles. Men always wished to touch her, and Daniel seemed no different.

But for Daniel, this moment was something entirely else. It was something sacred. He had always hoped for a chance to speak with her, to just *be* near her. And now, here she was, right in front of him. The sister of his friend's lover, in a world where such connections were almost convenient. In their society, it wasn't uncommon. Two sisters, two friends, it made dates easier, decisions simpler, stories easier to cover.

She was stunning. Her presence was magnetic. Daniel's thoughts raced.

What if I touched her hand?

Would she pull away? Would she be offended? Or would she let it happen?

Sonu, watching his stillness, wondered what was taking him so long.

Why's he just staring at me? she thought, amused.

If he wanted to kiss me, he could have done it a hundred times by now. Grapes aren't sour today, Daniel, they're sweet.

Suddenly, a loud noise came from above, a rhythmic thudding against the ceiling, unmistakable in its meaning.

They both burst into laughter.

There was no need to guess what was happening upstairs.

And in the warmth of that laughter, something shifted.

Daniel reached out gently and took Sonu's hand. She didn't resist. He pulled her slightly closer. Their faces drew near, close enough to hear each other's breath, feel the heat of the day trapped in their skin. The smell of sweat lingered between them, but in such moments, such things lose their offense. Desire has its own scent, and theirs was real.

Then, suddenly, Daniel kissed her.

A soft, nervous kiss, quick, almost innocent. Like a child who dares to poke a stranger and then runs away, giggling.

Sonu blinked.

Really? That's it?

Daniel pulled back, unsure. "Are you... angry?" he asked hesitantly.

"Why should I be angry?" she replied, tilting her head slightly.

"I thought... maybe you'd mind if I kissed you."

"If you *only* kiss me, and nothing more..." she said, teasingly, "then yes, I'll mind."

Her words lit something inside him. A bright gleam danced in his eyes, part disbelief, part joy.

That day became a memory neither of them would forget. If not Sonu, then certainly Daniel. For him, it was one of the best days of his life.

Moments later, Payja and Rani descended from the upper room. Both were drenched in sweat, their clothes clinging to them, eyes half-lidded with exhaustion and satisfaction.

No one said a word.

Some things didn't need saying.

That afternoon, as the heat of the day settled into a golden lull, Rani told Payja the news.

"I'm getting married," she said quietly, her eyes downcast, fingers nervously twisting the edge of her scarf. "To a relative. My mother arranged it."

Payja sat silently for a moment, looking at her face, still soft, still beautiful.

"I didn't want this," Rani added, her voice breaking slightly. "But you know… I'll still be yours. Always. Even if I belong to someone else in name, I'll remain your girlfriend, forever."

A flicker passed through Payja's eyes. He gave a small smile and nodded.

"Of course," he said.

Inside, however, he felt something closer to relief.

Rani was beautiful, no doubt. Young, vibrant, a pleasant distraction from the weight of daily life. But love? Commitment? No. Not in the way she imagined.

For Payja, this relationship had been nothing more than a shift in flavor, change of taste in a life often dulled by routine. A break from the demands of home. A place to breathe.

Like many men, Payja believed that marriage, once entered, changed everything. Wives became mothers. Romance became responsibility. The perfume and soft glances of courtship faded into tired routines. Makeup was replaced with the scent of cooking oil. Laughter was replaced with grocery lists. And the once-sensual whispers turned into complaints about bills, school fees, and the rising price of milk.

He had seen it too many times.

Before marriage, women dressed like dreams. They stayed fragrant, playful, seductive. After marriage, the same women became weary, practical, distant. They only dressed up to go outside. Inside the home, they wore exhaustion like a uniform.

Romance, in most marriages, didn't die, it was simply forgotten.

And so, men, like Payja, looked outside. Not necessarily because they stopped loving their wives, but because they missed the *girlfriend kind* of romance, the playfulness, the touch, the admiration. They missed being looked at with desire instead of obligation.

It was a quiet truth in many households.

So, when Rani said she was getting married, Payja's heart didn't break. It relaxed. Because he knew now, she wouldn't demand more. She wouldn't want a future, a place in his home, or a piece of his already complicated life. She'd stay in the shadows, where things were easier.

There was, after all, something particular about men. Many could hold extramarital affairs and still return home with loyalty in their own way. They didn't want to leave their wives. They didn't want to break their homes. They simply needed *something else* now and then, a different kind of warmth, a different kind of conversation. For most men, the role of a wife and that of a girlfriend were not the same. They weren't interchangeable.

A wife, they believed, should be responsible. Stable. The foundation of the house.

A girlfriend? She was the breeze, the perfume in the wind, the thrill of rebellion, the echo of youth.

Men saw these roles separately. Perhaps unfairly. Perhaps selfishly. But undeniably, it was how many lived and thought, even if they never said it aloud.

It was typical. And deeply human.

And difficult to explain.

Chapter 4

MAKING THE GOLD

It was time.

The night was heavy with silence, and a strange anticipation filled the air around Rana's house. A group of six men, Payja, Daniel, Rash, Rana, Kalu, and Baba, sat huddled together, their eyes sharp with the kind of hope that borders on madness.

They had decided to carry out the experiment in an abandoned house at the edge of the village. There were far enough curious eyes, hidden behind fields and tall grass, where no passerby would hear a sound or notice the glow of a fire in the dark.

This was a secret ritual. And there was one remaining.

The goal: to turn copper into gold.

They called it a *science of faith*. Part alchemy, part old-world wisdom, part desperation. No one truly knew if it would work, but the belief was strong enough to ignite fire and fire was exactly what they needed.

The ingredients were gathered carefully:

A gas cylinder, stolen from Rana's cousin's shed.

A sack full of dried *uplas*, cow dung cakes, used traditionally as fuel for cooking.

Copper pieces, cleaned and ready.

A handful of rare herbs.

And one dangerous addition: *Jamal Ghota*, a purging croton seed known for its violent potency. It was said to awaken the energy of transformation when used correctly.

But most importantly, they had *Hazardani*. Their treasure. The sacred herb.

Under a flickering lantern, Payja began the process. Every movement was slow, almost ceremonial.

He placed a layer of Hazardani inside a clay cooking basin, worn, blackened, used only for this. Then, he gently poured copper pieces over the herb, like a priest laying offerings on an altar.

Another layer of Hazardani followed, and then the lid. He sealed the basin with clay, pressing it firmly until no air could enter or escape.

The sealed basin was placed in the center of a pit surrounded by *uplas*. Then, with quiet reverence, they lit the fire.

The flames caught quickly, the dry fuel crackling, hissing, alive. The fire licked the basin's sides until the clay glowed red-hot, pulsing in the night like a beating heart.

No one spoke.

They watched in silence, their faces lit by flame and dreams. If the fire burned long enough, if the basin held through the night, and the ashes turned white, they would open it in the morning.

And perhaps…

Perhaps there would be gold.

Everyone there imagined their future already, houses, clothes, women, respect. Power.

But for now, they waited.

Six men. One dream.

And a fire in the dark that promised the impossible.

The clay pot sat in a cradle of white ash, its surface dull and cracked, still warm to the touch in the early morning breeze. The fire had long died, leaving behind only the silence of expectation.

Payja crouched beside the remnants of the night's experiment, carefully brushing aside the ash. The others gathered around him, Daniel, Rana, Kalu, Baba, and Rash, all wide-eyed with hope and fatigue. No one slept. They had all waited, watching the fire burn down to silence.

With steady hands, Payja lifted the pot and gently cracked the clay seal. A whisper of smoke rose as he opened it. Inside, the copper had changed, visibly.

It was no longer the same dull metal. Its surface was lit, taking on a pale, almost golden hue. It looked softer, brittle even, as if it had lost some of its weight. It flaked slightly at the edges, delicate and airy like dried petals.

But it was not gold.

Not yet.

The room remained silent for a moment, the weight of disappointment almost creeping in, until Payja spoke.

"This is just the first step," he said calmly. "It's working."

Daniel leaned closer. "It looks… different."

"It *is* different," Payja nodded. "But to make it gold, we need the second process. And that will take more time."

That day, they began the next phase, extracting the sacred water from another rare herb: *Satyanasi*. A humble plant, green and spiny, known more in village whispers than in books. It was believed to hold the purifying essence needed to complete the transformation.

But they would need a lot of it.

The entire group spread out across the countryside, gathering as much Satyanasi as they could find. By noon, their bags were full. Then began the real work, mashing the leaves, grinding them down by hand until they were nothing but pulp. It was laborious, slow, and sticky. Their fingers stained green, their arms aching.

Using old cotton cloth, they began squeezing the juice, drop by drop, into a clay pot.

One liter.

That was the goal.

It took the whole day.

By the time the sun dipped below the hills, they had it, the green liquid, glimmering faintly in the light, smelling sharp and bitter. This was no ordinary juice. It was the second ingredient in a recipe older than memory. The process was long, yes. But no one complained. Because something was happening.

The copper had already begun to change.

And the second stage had just begun.

They had at least one full liter of *Satyanasi* juice. A strange, almost luminous green liquid, sharp in scent and heavy in meaning. But the next step was crucial: the mixing of *Jamal Ghota*, the purging croton.

The seeds were dark and hard, potent and dangerous. Too much could poison a man. But in this process, they were sacred, an agent of change.

They poured a handful of the seeds into the juice, then began to crush them slowly using an old wooden pestle, the kind once used by their grandmothers to grind spices or mix dough. It wasn't easy. The seeds resisted, oily and tough. But with each turn of the pestle, the mixture thickened, darkened, took on a deeper presence.

They worked in silence.

No one joked. No one smoked. The fire nearby crackled in the dark, casting long shadows against the mud-brick walls. The night had grown dense and quiet, as if even the wind was watching them.

In the center of their circle, they lit a small jeweler's furnace, a handmade clay crucible used by goldsmiths. The fire underneath it hissed with steady breath as they prepared to melt the copper they had altered the night before.

The process was simple in theory but exhausting in practice.

Melt the copper.

Pour it into the Satyanasi-Jamal Ghota mixture.

Let it cool.

Repeat.

Seventy-two times.

Each cycle, an offering to the unknown.

Each repetition, a prayer disguised as labor.

Payja lifted the first chunk of copper with tongs and lowered it into the tiny furnace. They all leaned in, watching it change shape, hard edges softening, turning to liquid. When it glowed bright like molten sun, he quickly poured it into the cold herbal mix.

A sharp hiss. Steam. A pungent smell rising into the night.

Then again.

And again.

They worked like monks performing sacred rites. Time blurred. The night stretched long, and their faces, lit by the fire, grew worn with smoke and hope.

But none of them wavered.

They believed it.

If they could complete this, if they could endure all 72 cycles, then the copper, reborn through fire and herb, would become something else entirely.

Gold.

Not just metal, but *freedom*. The power to reshape their lives.

And so, under the gaze of stars and the watch of shadows, they kept going.

One burn at a time.

The night dragged on like a slow-burning prayer. They took turns tending to the fire, each man stepping in and out like monks in a temple of smoke and flame. One would take over the stirring, while another slipped out to smoke, to rest, to relieve himself. But the work never stopped.

Cycle after cycle, they fed the crucible. Melted the copper. Dipped it into a sacred mixture. Then again. And again.

By the time they crossed the fiftieth round, the copper had begun to change. It no longer looked like itself. It shimmered faintly; its color softened into something luminous, like gold bathed in early sunlight. The texture, once firm and stubborn, now felt tender under their touch.

They were close. So close.

The sky was beginning to change, pale blue bleeding into the black as dawn approached. A cold wind swept in and then came the whisper none of them wanted to hear.

"The gas is almost finished," said Rana, his voice low.

Payja checked the flame, it had weakened. Fading.

"No," Baba muttered. "Not now."

But the truth came sharp and final: the cylinder hissed once… and died.

The fire was gone.

They stood around it in silence. The copper for the 70th step was cooling fast, and without fire, they couldn't melt it again. They had no backup cylinder. No wood ready to burn. Nothing.

Just two steps away.

Two.

The piece of metal in Payja's hand was beautiful. It shone with the color of gold, warm and soft and full of promise.

"I think we've done it," someone whispered. "It *looks* like gold."

"It feels like gold," another added.

Payja looked at the others, holding the lump of hope between his fingers. "Should we test it in acid?"

They all knew the risk. The old way to test gold, nitric acid. If it was real, it would survive. Sit calmly beneath the acid, unshaken. And when water was poured in, the gold would rise from the base like a phoenix from ashes.

But if it was still copper…

The acid would devour it. And nothing would come back.

It was a gamble.

A dangerous one.

They hadn't completed all 72 steps.

But hope, and ego, whispered in their ears.

"It's only two steps short," said Baba. "It *must* be ready."

Everyone nodded. A heavy, reluctant agreement.

Payja dropped the piece into the nitric acid.

They watched.

It fizzled.

It hissed.

And then… it vanished.

Gone.

Silence.

Like death in the room.

It wasn't gold.

It had never been gold.

"What did we do?" whispered Daniel, barely able to speak. "Why didn't we wait… just wait for more gas?"

"We were *so close*," said Rana, his voice cracking.

Now they'd have to start all over again.

New copper.

More *Hazardani*.

More *Satyanasi*.

More *Jamal Ghota*.

All of it. Again.

The room grew heavy. Smoke, regret, and silence coiled in the corners like ghosts.

They had chased gold.

Touched it, almost.

And then watched it dissolve.

A dream undone by impatience.

And for the first time that night, no one spoke.

Only the ashes of the fire, still warm, remembered how close they had come.

When the morning child rose, sunlight slipping through the cracks of the broken windows, they could finally see each other clearly in the cold, sobering light of day.

Their faces were heavy with sleep, smoke, and failure.

But something else was wrong.

Rash's nose was unusually red, puffed like a balloon. Kala squinted at him, then looked down at himself and frowned.

"My... my balls," he said, stunned. "They've swollen up."

Payja checked himself too, pulling at his waistband with a confused grimace.

"What the hell?" he muttered. "Why is *that* bigger?"

Then it hit them all.

The *Jamal Ghota*.

The purging croton.

They had worked the entire night without gloves, their bare hands soaked in the thick herbal mixture. They had wiped sweat from their brows, scratched their faces, rubbed their eyes... and, worst of all, gone to pee.

They had unknowingly transferred the harsh, burning irritant to every sensitive part of their bodies.

"Oh God, what *is* this?!" shouted Daniel, horrified.

"This is what happens when you do experiments without any damn sense," he continued, pacing furiously. "You need to *know* what you're working with, what effects these herbs can have on your health. We're lucky it's only swelling. It could have been worse."

They all groaned, shifting uncomfortably, trying to hide their burning embarrassment beneath their already burning skin.

Daniel wasn't done.

"And another thing," he said, now fully in philosopher mode. "Patience. It's the key to everything. You can run faster than everyone in a race, but if you stop just before the finish line, what does it matter? You didn't win. You failed. You need to endure till the *end*. That's how success works, makes effort, continuous effort, and crossing the line. That's when it counts."

"Shut up, you philosopher," Payja snapped, still holding his groin. "We're already suffering. Don't pour kerosene on the fire."

No one laughed.

Defeated, swollen, and half-cooked by their own mistake, they each picked up their things and headed home, limping, itching, and stung not just by the croton… but by the bitterness of almost becoming legends.

Chapter 5

DIFFERENT DIRECTIONS

As Rani's wedding day crept closer, she found herself visiting Payja's village more often. The town had better shops, fabric stalls bursting with colors, glass bangles that shimmered like raindrops, and small jewelry stores tucked in alleys that smelled of dust and perfume.

Each time she went shopping, Sonu came with her. It had become their unspoken ritual, first a visit to Payja's house, then the marketplace. They laughed, they flirted, they stole glances and touches as if nothing in the world was changing.

Rani was set to marry someone else. But her connection with Payja hadn't dimmed. If anything, it burned stronger under the weight of time running out. She knew she wouldn't stop seeing him, not even after marriage. He had become her comfort, her thrill, her anchor.

And Sonu? She had quietly accepted her bond with Daniel. There wasn't much choice; he was always there. And over time, Daniel's calm presence, his respectful silences, and soft curiosity made her feel seen. It wasn't love. Not yet. But it was something. And for now, that was enough.

One afternoon, as the sun cast soft gold over the rooftops and the sounds of wedding drums could already be heard from distant homes, Rani sat with Payja in his small room.

"You know, Payja," she said, brushing her fingers along a thread of embroidery in her shawl, "my wedding is next week."

Payja nodded, his face unreadable.

"I want to tell you something important," she added, her voice barely above a whisper.

He looked up. "Okay… I'm listening."

Rani took a breath. Her eyes didn't meet his.

"Actually… I'm pregnant."

The words dropped like a stone into a still pond. For a second, everything around them stopped.

"What?" Payja blinked, the ground under his feet suddenly unstable. He gripped a nearby stool to steady himself, the color draining from his face.

"How?"

Rani looked at him, finally meeting his eyes.

"Don't ask me that. You know how. It's not something I did alone, Payja."

Silence.

But her voice remained calm.

"Don't worry. I'm getting married next week. There won't be any problem. It'll be fine."

Payja opened his mouth to speak, then paused. Something had caught in his throat.

"But what if…" he began but stopped halfway.

"What if *what*?" Rani asked, gently.

There was no fear in her tone. No panic. Just a quiet strength. A woman who had accepted the mess, the risk, and still chose to walk forward.

"There won't be anything wrong," she said. "Just trust me."

Payja exhaled slowly, letting the silence settle between them again.

"Alright," he said finally. "If you don't have a problem with it... I don't either."

And that was all.

No promises.

No guarantees.

Just the truth, raw and unpolished, sitting between them like a secret too big to be spoken again.

This is the naked truth of our society, of regions like India and Pakistan, where love is often more dangerous than hate. Where morality, honor, and religion stand taller than compassion. And in the middle of it all, the burden almost always falls on the woman.

In relationships, real or performed, when things go beyond the lines society has drawn, when desire becomes action, and love becomes intimacy, consequences arrive swiftly and silently. Pregnancy, in such a context, isn't just a biological event, it's a *crime*, a scarlet letter stitched into a woman's skin.

Thousands of young women bear this burden alone. Some carry the child in silence. Some give birth and throw their newborns away in the dead of night. Some hand their babies to strangers and vanish. Because to be a mother without a marriage certificate is to be declared immoral. A sinner.

If the pregnancy is detected early, they rush for abortions, quiet, secret, illegal. If detected too late, desperation forces them into back-alley clinics, where the procedure becomes life-threatening. Many never return. And when they die, they are still blamed. No one mourns. No one questions the boy, the man, the partner. The shame is hers. The blood is hers.

In deeply religious families, especially Muslim households, girls have no choice. If their secret is discovered, their life is at risk not metaphorically, but *literally*. Fathers, brothers, those sworn to protect, may become executioners. Honor killings are real. Countless daughters have been murdered in the name of religion, respect, and family pride.

Isn't it strange? That even after centuries on this earth... after discoveries, revolutions, education, enlightenment, human beings still cannot accept something as basic as desire?

It is a universal truth: when a man and woman grow into adulthood, they develop needs. Bodily, emotional, sexual needs. It is natural. It is human. And it should not be a death sentence.

With proper education and awareness, so many lives could be saved. So many futures protected. But society, blinded by rules older than its own language, chooses punishment over understanding.

Religions that are thousands of years old still govern minds shaped by modern science and psychology. Those ancient laws were born in a time when the human body was misunderstood, when mental illness was called demon-possession, when hysteria in women was treated with violence or rushed marriages. And oddly enough, marriage was often the *cure*, not because it healed the woman, but because it allowed sex to be socially accepted.

Today, we know better.

We understand the mind. We understand the body. We understand what repression does to the human spirit.

The denial of sexual needs doesn't make a person holy; it makes them ill. Anxious. Angry. Sick. Especially for young girls and boys, this suppression turns into lifelong trauma, shame, and emotional instability.

It's time societies wake up and teach, not preach.

Teach the young how to fulfill their desires safely, without harm. Teach them love, not fear. Trust, not silence. Empower them with knowledge so they don't have to choose between shame and survival.

Because without change, this story will keep repeating.

And too many voices will go unheard.

There is another truth, unwritten, unspoken, yet lived by countless souls, that remains hidden beneath the surface of societies like ours. The truth is so ordinary, it's become invisible. And yet, it wrecks lives from the inside out.

It is the truth of *misaligned love*.

Of falling in love with one person and marrying another.

It happens every day.

It happened to Rani. It happened to Payja.

Rani, out of need, for safety, for stability, chose to marry a man she did not love. A man she barely knew. And yet, she held onto Payja, the man who made her feel alive. The man who wasn't hers to begin with.

And Payja, he didn't love her either. He knew it. But he lacked the courage to say it. He enjoyed her beauty, her body, the thrill of their secrecy. She was a taste in his otherwise stale life. Nothing more.

Both knew the truth.

And both lacked the courage to face it.

This moral silence, this absence of clarity, this *fear* of truth, is where so many stories go wrong.

And then comes the third man. The one Rani will marry. A financially stable, perhaps kind but simple man who knows little about her heart. He sees her beauty and believes it's meant for him, not realizing that beauty doesn't follow wealth, it follows connection. But in our societies, wealth often wins the bride.

It's strange, isn't it? How many beautiful women marry men who are twice their age, lacking charm or presence, and whose only virtue is a bank account. And still, we call that a *successful match.*

No one asks: *Why is she marrying him?*

No one wants to hear the answer.

Because the answer is too simple.

Security.

And what happens next is the quiet tragedy.

Many of these marriages carry another man's shadow.

Children are born from secret love affairs. Wives who carry guilt in silence. Husbands who think they've won but never ask themselves why they feel like strangers in their own homes.

These truths are not rare, they are *normal.*

But our silence keeps them hidden.

We judge women like Rani for being with a married man.

We don't ask *why* she chose him.

We don't ask *why* she can't leave him.

We don't ask *why* she has no choice but to marry someone else.

And we never judge men like Payja, who take and take, without responsibility.

This is the tragedy:

That in the name of family, reputation, and so-called honor, people live lives that are not their own.

They lie to themselves.

They marry wrong.

They love wrong.

And worst of all, they pretend it's okay.

It was a hot, breathless day. The kind of day when the sun doesn't just burn, it lingers in the skin, sticks to your clothes, and makes every moment feel heavier than it should.

And it was the day Rani was to be married.

To a man she did not love but had accepted as her husband.

In villages across the Indo-Pak region, this is not an uncommon story, love quietly sacrificed at the altar of duty, security, and silence. What's spoken in private is buried in public. And what lives in the heart is traded for a name, a roof, and a socially acceptable future.

Payja and Daniel, who were frequent visitors to Rani's village and well known to her family under the safe label of "old friends," had been invited to the wedding. Her mother, Fatima, had always accepted Payja's presence with a knowing smile. In the eyes of the village, they were close family friends. Nothing more.

In this part of the world, such scenes are familiar, *boyfriends working like brothers at their lovers' weddings*. Disguised in duty. Hidden in plain sight.

Weddings here are events that swallow entire days and half the village. Chairs need arranging, food needs serving, water must be poured, drinks passed, guests greeted. There is always work. Always need hands.

And so Payja worked.

"Come on, set those chairs up properly," Daniel said with a sly grin, wiping sweat from his brow. "It's your sister's wedding, after all. Let's get moving, guests are almost here!"

"Shut up," muttered Payja under his breath, not even looking up.

Daniel laughed, stepping back with mock innocence. "Fine. But your turn is coming too. I'll be setting up chairs at *your* sister Sonu's wedding one day. Just wait."

Payja smirked, his pride hurt, his heart heavier than he'd admitted.

A shout came from the gate.

"They're here!" someone called out, pointing toward the village crossing. "The *baraat* is coming!"

People began gathering near the entrance to the street. The *baraat*, the wedding procession—had arrived. A long trail of men and women followed the groom, dressed in glittering clothes and celebration. In this culture, a groom never arrives alone. He is surrounded by a small army: friends, uncles, cousins, neighbors, anywhere from a hundred to two hundred guests, singing, laughing, and celebrating.

It is the bride's family's responsibility to receive them.

Food, drinks, endless hospitality, it all begins the moment the *baraat* enters the home.

Soon, the legal ceremony would begin. The religious ritual, whether led by a priest, a mullah, or a pandit, would formally tie Rani to her groom. A few sacred words would be uttered, blessings whispered, and just like that, a girl's life would be altered forever.

And Rani?

Somewhere inside, hidden behind layers of jewelry and painted smiles, she was preparing to marry a stranger.

While the man she had once loved passed cups of water to guests and folded plastic chairs in the burning sun.

The groom arrived surrounded by his *baraat*, swaying awkwardly under the heat, dressed in golden silk that did little to improve his strange appearance. A dark-skinned man with large, twitchy eyes behind thick glasses, he looked like someone who could barely stand still for a moment, nervous, uncertain, lost.

"What bad luck for the bride," someone whispered from the crowd, shaking their head.

"Bad luck?" replied another. "She's lucky, she'll have everything. A big house, servants, money, freedom."

"Still," the first voice sighed, "it's not a good match."

"Who looks at a match these days?" the second voice chuckled bitterly. "People follow wealth now."

Soon after, the groom was led inside, into the decorated room where Rani sat with her head lowered. A local *Mullah* entered with calm authority and began the *Nikah*, the wedding ceremony. Before two witnesses, the bride and groom exchanged their silent acceptance.

"*Qubool hai.*"

Three times spoken, and it was done.

Just like that, with a few ritual words, two strangers were declared husband and wife.

Guests prayed aloud, blessings filled the room, and sweets were passed around, dry dates and sugar candies, as tradition demands, sweetening the bitterness of what is never spoken.

Several ceremonies followed: laughter, photographs, and heavy food. But beneath it all was the silence of a woman accepting a future not of her choosing.

Then came the *rukhsati*, the departure.

The moment every wedding builds toward.

In older times, the bride would be lifted in a cradle or wooden palanquin by her brothers or father, carried out of her home and into the unknown. Now, she is seated in a decorated car, adorned like a gift wrapped for delivery. But one tradition has not changed:

She must cry.

Loud, visible, undeniable tears. It is both custom and performance. In some cases, real. In others, rehearsed. But always expected.

In many Indo-Pak marriages, brides don't truly know the men they're marrying. The tears are not just cultural, they are genuine fear. Because the moment she leaves home, she steps into a life she cannot undo.

So, Rani cried.

She cried for her mother, her protector, her guide, the one who had held her hand through everything. And she cried for something else… for someone else.

Payja.

She looked at him one last time through her blurred eyes and knew: there would be no family, no shared life, no open path with him now. If she wanted him, it would no longer be a love story, it would be an affair. A sin. From this day on, being with Payja would require secrecy, lies, and guilt.

Just one word, *Qubool hai,* had changed everything.

A single, quiet acceptance before a Mullah and two witnesses had handed her to another man.

And with that, he now had the right to her body, her time, her identity. Whether she desired him or not. Whether he understood her or not. Whether love existed or not.

Marriage had made it all *permissible.*

The man, awkward and unfamiliar, now had the right to sleep beside her. To touch her. To expect things. She, in return, would be expected to adjust, to serving, to fulfill roles she never chose.

And somehow, this is called sacred.

When a man and woman are not married, the world watches them like criminals for even holding hands. But once married, society gives them a license to do everything, even if one of them resists, even if neither of them is ready. Consent is no longer questioned, because marriage *assumes* it.

And while all of this is accepted without thinking, the one thing they must never do again, under any circumstance, is seek love outside the marriage. No matter how loveless the bond may be. No matter how mismatched.

This is the contradiction no one dares to name.

The holy bond of marriage, so often built on compromise, silence, performance, binds two people tighter than chains. And for a woman, especially, it is more than a contract. It becomes her new identity. Her limit. Her cage.

Rani cried.

Not just for what she was leaving.

But for what she was walking into.

Chapter 6

THE SAINT

Daniel had always known, deep inside, that their gold-making experiments would never really succeed. But he had stayed with Payja and the others, not for the gold, but for the journey. In a small, stagnant village, these mad pursuits were the only taste of adventure he had.

And though the others were growing weary, none of them had lost anything, except for Payja, who had been pouring his savings into herbs, tools, and hope. Some of that funding even came from Pa Shida, Payja's distant relative and Daniel's occasional host in the border village of *Bara Manga*, a quiet, green place wrapped in mystery and wind.

Most of their nights in Bara Manga were spent in deep conversation, surrounded by the scent of firewood and crushed herbs.

"You know, Payja," Pa Shida said one evening, grinding something dark with a stone, "we need to find *Black Sunkhya*. I went all the way to Lahore, but I couldn't find the real stuff. Even poisons these days are fake."

"That's the problem," said Payja, exhaling smoke. "Even poison isn't pure anymore."

"I think we need someone from India," Pa Shida added. "They still have original herbs, minerals. Everything is available across the border."

"But trade's closed," Payja replied bitterly. "No official links. No permission. No exchange. The idiots in uniform have made sure of that."

Daniel sat quietly at first, then leaned forward.

"Of course," he said. "Peace is dangerous for them. If India and Pakistan ever become friends, the generals will be unemployed. Their empires, mansions, factories, and personal airlines, all built on hate. They cook their food on the fire of war. They *need* it to keep burning."

"There are three classes in this country now," Daniel continued. "The rich. The poor. And the army. People know the rich and the poor, but no one dares speak of the third."

"They live behind walls," he said, his voice growing colder. "They have their own hospitals, their own schools, their own cinemas, their own cities, cantonments where no ordinary civilian can walk freely. Their kids don't sit with yours in classrooms. Their families don't wait in the same lines. And it's all funded by one source: *us*."

"We came here by bus, didn't we?" he turned to Payja. "That bus runs on diesel. Every liter you buy, more than 100% tax. Same with sugar, flour, beans, every bite we eat has tax hidden in its price. Even the cigarette you smoke."

"I don't pay tax on cigarettes," said Payja casually. "I pay the price."

Daniel held out his hand. "Give me your pack."

Payja handed it over.

"Look here," Daniel pointed. "Price: 100 rupees. Tax included: 20. You're not paying 100 for a cigarette, you're paying 80 for the product and 20 to fuel the army's jeeps.

Payja frowned. "So, we pay for their guns?"

"Not just guns," Daniel replied. "Private helicopters. Foreign hotel bills. Imported boots and toilet paper. Every time you light a cigarette; you're paying for someone's luxurious piss in Paris."

"Damn," muttered Payja.

"And the worst part?" Daniel's voice darkened. "They don't let civilians build anything. No real democracy. Politicians are kept weak on purpose, so they can be blackmailed, used, thrown away."

"They make sure politicians are corrupt, so they can control them. They use media to paint themselves as saviors and politicians as thieves. It's all propaganda. And the people? They believe it. They even *thank* their abusers."

Daniel paused, his voice soft now.

"If there were peace between India and Pakistan… people wouldn't be running after gold in caves or grinding herbs in the dark. They'd have real jobs. Real futures. The poor wouldn't need to steal, and the rich wouldn't need to bribe."

"But peace," he added, "would destroy the generals' profits. And worse, peace would open the eyes of this nation."

He fell silent.

The fire cracked in the dark, the flame reflecting in their tired eyes.

Daniel leaned back, the firelight flickering in his eyes. The night in Bara Manga had grown deeper, the air dense with smoke, herbs, and heavy truths.

"You know what bothers me the most?" Daniel said suddenly, his tone serious. "Every time we open a newspaper, every time we switch on the television, it's the *Chief of Army Staff* speaking."

"He's telling us how to fix the economy. He's talking about inflation. He's giving statements about floods, earthquakes, education, terrorism, even religion. One man, *a soldier* is speaking like he's the oracle of this nation."

He paused, letting it sink in.

"But the only thing he doesn't seem to know," Daniel said with a bitter smile, "is how to defend this country."

Payja looked at him, eyebrows raised.

"Our country lost every war," Daniel continued. "We lost Kashmir. We lost Siachen. We lost Kargil. And we lost half the country, Bangladesh. You remember the surrender? Their pants were taken off, literally. A whole army brought down to their knees in front of the world."

"All those war heroes we're taught to worship, they're not heroes. They're fairy tales. Stories we were fed like gospel. And no one dares to say otherwise. Because we've been told these men are *patriots*, defenders of faith and country. But in reality..." Daniel's voice lowered. "They're the cruelest animals walking this land."

Payja blinked. "Why do you hate your own army so much?"

Daniel looked at him, not with anger, but with clarity.

"I don't hate our army. I respect every jawan standing at the border. Every soldier risks his life. But I hate the *generals*. The one in designer suits, not uniforms. The ones flying in private choppers while a child dies of hunger. The ones who've forgotten their job."

He leaned forward; eyes locked with Payja's.

"The job of the army is simple: *follow orders*. Orders of a civilian government. Defend the land when *they* say so. That's it. They're not kings. They're not messiahs. And they're not economists or religious scholars."

"Have you ever heard the name of the Chief of Army Staff of India?" Daniel asked, voice sharp now. "Or the United States? Germany? France? Iran? Saudi Arabia?"

Payja frowned, thinking hard. "Oye... no. I haven't."

"Exactly," Daniel said, triumphant. "That's the point. In no other country do army chiefs give weekly press conferences. No other country allows soldiers to play politics and preach to the people through media like prophets."

"And yet, in our land, they're everywhere. On billboards. On channels. In textbooks. They run banks, hospitals, housing societies, factories, even schools. And we call it patriotism."

He looked into the flames, quieter now.

"True patriotism is letting the people choose. Letting democracy grow. Letting the constitution breathe."

"But in our country, the generals are the landlords, and we are the cattle."

The fire crackled gently in the corner as Pa Shida brought in a kettle of fresh tea. Steam rose softly, carrying the scent of cardamom and earth. The three men, Pa Shida, Payja, and Daniel, sat in silence, wrapped in their thoughts, the smoke from their past failures still hanging in the air like the thin veil between hope and reality.

Pa Shida, older and weathered, had spent years chasing gold, not for wealth, but for understanding. He had poured millions into his experiments over the years, thanks to the steady income from his large agricultural land. He believed, as Payja and Daniel did in their hearts, that they were alchemists, not scientists, not frauds, but seekers.

They followed whispers, ancient manuscripts, and half-remembered stories passed from one dreamer to another. Like so many alchemists before them, they knew failure was part of the path. Some men had spent their whole lives in search of gold and died empty-handed, but their notes, their fire, had passed on.

"Payja," Pa Shida finally broke the silence, "if we could go to India, just once there's one experiment, I know we need to try. After that, I believe we'll succeed."

Payja and Daniel leaned forward, their tea forgotten.

"There was a saint," Pa Shida began, eyes glinting with memory. "He travelled the entire length of India, from the Himalayas to Kanyakumari. He lived among *Sanyasis*, learned from them, studied ancient alchemy. Then, one day, he disappeared into a cave."

"He stayed there for a year. Alone. Silent. No one knew what he did inside that cave. But when he came out, he had one kilo of gold in his hand. He walked to the nearest town and went to a goldsmith. Told him he wanted to sell it."

"The goldsmith, surprised by the purity, asked how much he wanted. But the saint said, 'Give me only what you have today. We can talk about the rest later.'"

The goldsmith, respectful and a little stunned, gave him a portion of the money and offered food and hospitality. He even asked the saint to stay in his spare house, but the saint declined.

'I prefer my cave,' he said with a smile. 'But you may visit me there.'

He took the money and left.

A week has passed. The saint never returned to claim the rest of the money.

So, the goldsmith packed a basket with fruits, sweets, groceries, and the remaining gold payment. He walked to the cave the saint had spoken of.

Smoke was rising from inside.

Outside, the saint sat peacefully, watching the flames as something glowed red-hot in a small clay crucible. The goldsmith approached and greeted him.

But the saint looked at him, puzzled. "Have we met?"

"I'm the goldsmith," he replied. "You sold me the gold last week. I brought you the rest of your money."

The saint smiled but showed no memory of the exchange. Yet, he welcomed him warmly. "Ah, good," he said. "I was about to head to the village to buy food. You saved me the trip."

The goldsmith didn't press further. He simply observed the burning pot in the fire, silent, glowing.

Then the saint turned to him.

"Would you help me sometimes?" he asked.

"Of course," the goldsmith replied without hesitation. "Just tell me how."

The saint reached into his robe and handed him a small, folded paper. "These are some minerals and chemicals I need. If you can bring them next time, that would be enough."

The goldsmith glanced at the list, then at the saint. "But this isn't expensive. What will you do with the money I brought?"

The saint handed all of it back to him.

"I don't need it," he said softly. "You've already given me what I need to live here. I don't eat money."

And in that moment, the goldsmith understood, this was no ordinary man.

He accepted the paper and the money, bowed gently, and left in silence.

"You know," Pa Shida said, leaning forward, "the goldsmith… he went to buy those things right away. He never asked questions. He understood something few ever do, that the saint wasn't just making gold. He *was* gold."

The goldsmith had long been a simple man, honest, respected, with a thriving business in his village. But meeting the saint changed his life. He began to visit regularly, at different times of the day, bringing food, minerals, and the supplies requested. He never demanded answers. He never questioned the fire or the crucibles or the sealed clay pots.

Sometimes, he saw the saint crushing herbs with minerals. Sometimes, melt copper in small pots. Sometimes, sealing something under *uplas* and setting fire all around.

But the saint never opened the pots in his presence.

And still, he would hand the goldsmith pieces of gold. "Sell this," he would say softly. "Bring me what I need."

The goldsmith obeyed, and his business grew beyond his imagination. Wealth flowed into his life. But the saint never accepted money. He never left the cave. No matter how many times the goldsmith offered a home, comfort, servants, he refused it all.

Then, one day, the goldsmith came and found the saint weakened, pale, barely able to breathe. His body was fading, but his eyes still carried a light far beyond this world.

"I will not live long," the saint whispered, "but before I go, there is something you must know."

The goldsmith knelt beside him, silent.

"You are honest," the saint said. "And loyal. That's why I choose you. This path must not end with me. *Alchemy must live on.*"

He paused to breathe.

"I travelled," he said, voice cracking, "from Kashmir to Kanyakumari. I followed the steps of Mahadev. I meditated at Shankaracharya in Srinagar, then walked barefoot to Badrinath, Kedarnath, Dwarka, Rameswaram, and Puri. Every step was a prayer. Every night, a fire under the stars."

"I had no food unless someone gave it. No shelter but trees and caves. Hunger and thirst became strangers to me. Time vanished. Mahadev became everything. He was in my blood, my breath, my bones."

His eyes flickered with ancient memories.

"My senses sharpened. I could see farther than sight. Smell the coming of rain. Hear the whisper of ants. I could sense the shadow of death before it arrived. I was not human anymore. I was *open.*"

The goldsmith sat still, stunned.

"One night, while meditating, I saw Him."

His voice trembled.

"A figure of blue, with a cobra wrapped around His neck. Mahadev stood before me. I was not expecting Him, but there He was."

"He said, '*I am happy with you, my child. I know what you are looking for. Tell me, what blessing shall I grant you?*'"

"I had forgotten why I began. I didn't want anything anymore. I said, 'Mahadev, I am complete. I need nothing. Seeing You is more than all gold.'"

Mahadev smiled.

'But you once desired gold. You were an alchemist before you became a seeker. I will give you the senses to solve any mystery, to unlock any secret. If you wish, you can complete your work. You may now turn copper into gold.'

"I said no. I am happy."

Katastu.

He smiled.

And disappeared.

"I never tried," the saint said softly. "For a long time, I didn't want to."

"But one day," he continued, "I began to feel it again. A knowing in the soul. I remembered the formula, not from books, but from within. From visions."

"It needed four poisons," he whispered. "And the water of twenty-two *kunds*."

"I found *Jeevani Booti* on the slopes of the Himalayas, and when I mixed it with the four poisons, placed it in a clay pot, burned it under the *uplas* fire, as you saw, and then cooled it in the sacred water of twenty-two kunds… it became gold."

The saint's voice trembled now, weaker than before, but the goldsmith did not interrupt him. He could feel it, this man, who had carried the light of a thousand suns, was now slowly slipping into the unknown.

And yet, he continued to speak.

"When the gold finally appeared before me," the saint whispered, "I felt… nothing. No joy. No surprise. No triumph."

"To me, it was no more than dust on the road, or the grass beneath my feet. Something ordinary. Something meaningless."

He paused, his breath shallow.

"Many, many years ago, when I began this path, it was all I could think of, gold. To make it, to hold it. And for the first few years, that desire drove me. Then, slowly, I forgot it. Other things became more important. Then came silence, solitude, vision… until I found myself lost in the Nowhere."

"I gained control over dreams. Over thought. Over myself. Everything I could once wish for, I already had within me."

He closed his eyes briefly, then opened them again.

"And when I no longer needed any *vardan*, any blessing, Mahadev gave it to me."

A silence passed like wind between trees.

"It was strange… in that moment, the blessing felt useless. The most beautiful feeling I knew then was to melt into Mahadev, to merge into his presence, to be taken into *Shiv Lok*, to dissolve in his name forever."

"But he smiled within me. He knew."

The saint smiled now too, faint and slow.

"He gave me the very blessing I had once craved, when I no longer cared to ask for it. I began again, curious. *What now?* I wondered. And I realized, I did have one final wish. Not for gold. But for *him*. To live in Shiv Lok, forever, near the Lord of the Dance."

He coughed slightly. His voice was growing weaker.

"I didn't stop walking. I carried the gold with me. I didn't sell it. I didn't use it. One day, I passed through a village. On the bank of a river, I saw a man."

"My feet stopped."

The goldsmith listened, barely breathing.

"This man… he was scooping water in his palms, giving it to a dying dog. The sun was hot. The dog could barely breathe. And the man… he wasn't just helping; he *was* help itself."

"I sat under a tree nearby. Watched. The man left. Then he returned, carrying food. He placed it gently before the dog, dressed its wounds, and left again. I stayed for a few days. The man kept coming. The dog healed."

"One day, I saw the two walks together toward the village."

The saint's eyes shimmered.

"He lived in a small house. I saw birds there. Animals. Broken, injured, forgotten creatures he'd taken in. His wife, his child, they helped him, joyfully."

"Then, I saw him feed an old man who had been abandoned by his own son. He gave him medicine. Food. Company."

"Mahadev whispered inside me: *Give him what you have.*"

The saint looked at the goldsmith now, eyes heavy with the weight of love.

"I did."

The goldsmith felt something rise in his throat, and tears welled in his eyes. He understood.

The man… was him.

"I gave him the gold," the saint said. "And I watched him. Even with more than ever before, he never changed. He continued to serve."

The saint smiled; breath ragged.

"And the rest… you already know."

With those final words, the saint's body stilled.

His breath faded.

A strange calm filled the cave, as if the sky itself had stopped listening.

He had left this world, but his soul had risen into the *Shiv Lok*, forever in the presence of Mahadev.

The goldsmith wept, not for the saint's death, but for the gift he had received: not gold… but purpose.

The room had gone still. Even though the fire seemed to quiet down as Pa Shida spoke, his voice soaked in both mystery and memory.

"This goldsmith," he said, "lived a good life. Rich, respected. He never misused what the saint gave him. But one day, he died in an accident. Years later, his son, while going through his old things, found some papers tucked away in a hidden compartment of his locker."

Pa Shida paused, letting the weight of the story settle.

"He tried to replicate the experiments. He followed the instructions, but there was one thing he could never understand. One thing he could never find."

Everyone leaned in.

"The water of twenty-two kunds."

"He didn't even know what it meant. And I've searched everywhere across all of Pakistan. Asked every scholar, every saint, every herbalist I could find. No one knows. No one's even heard of it."

Daniel looked into the fire, thinking.

"How do *you* know this story is real?" asked Payja softly.

Pa Shida smiled. "Because the goldsmith's grandson is married to my wife's sister. We're family. They live in a small village near the border. And he showed me those same papers."

He leaned back, his eyes sharp.

"And that, my friends, is why I called you here."

"Aha!" Payja said, laughing. "So, *this* was your real reason."

"Yes," Pa Shida replied with a nod. "I didn't want to tell you until I told you the full story."

"But who will go to India?" he asked, glancing around the room. "We need someone with a sharp mind. Someone who can handle travel, strangers, language, and patience. Someone who won't get lost in the chaos of that land."

There was a pause.

Then Payja spoke. "There's only one person among us who can do that."

Everyone turned toward Daniel.

"He's right," said Rana. "Daniel is intelligent. Quiet. He listens. Observes. If anyone can find these things, it's him."

Kala nodded. "And he's fearless. If he goes, he'll come back with something."

All eyes were on Daniel.

Daniel didn't speak for a long moment. Then he looked at Pa Shida and said, "How much time it takes doesn't matter. How much money it costs doesn't matter. If you all believe it's worth it, then I'll go."

The room lit up with approval.

Everyone agreed.

Here, in this quiet room filled with smoke and silence, they sealed the pact. When Daniel returned with the four poisons, the *Jeevani Booti*, and the sacred water of twenty-two *kunds*, they would gather again, right here, in this place, and perform the final experiment.

Together.

Chapter 7

THE NEW FAMILY

When Rani stepped into her new home, it felt like entering a dream, one she had never dared to imagine for herself. The house was grand, almost palatial, with tall ceilings and walls dressed in silk and gold. Rich velvet curtains swayed gently in the evening air, and the bed in the center of the master room was adorned in red and gold, carefully decorated for the first night, as per tradition in many Asian cultures.

All around her, the mansion echoed with celebration. Guests were feasting, music played on every corner, and some people danced freely. Despite the country's conservative norms, alcohol flowed openly, because in wealthy families, Rani thought, *rules don't matter. Religion doesn't matter. Money writes its own laws.*

Everyone in the house shimmered. Her husband's sister was dressed like royalty, and the entire family glowed with extravagance, silks, diamonds, perfume, elegance. Though Rani did not find Hashmat, her husband, physically appealing, the house enchanted her. It was beyond anything she had ever known.

I'm the queen now, she thought. *The queen of this palace.*

"Come and sit, dear," said a woman in an elaborate sari. "I am your new mother, Hashmat's mother," she added with a warm smile. "And this is my daughter, Bisma."

One by one, the women of the house came to greet her. Each placed currency notes into her palm, *shagun*, the ritual gift for new brides. Soon, her hands were full. Rani had never held so much cash in her life. These were not small bills. All large denominations. Hundreds. Thousands.

She remembered how, just a month ago, she had gone to visit her friend Saima on her wedding day and had slipped only a five-rupee note into her hand, embarrassed but helpless. Poor brides received what people could spare. Sometimes, even on empty envelopes, no one watches closely enough to care.

But today, she wasn't that girl anymore.

She was the bride of a millionaire.

The night deepened, and the guests began to leave. Someone called out, "Let's go! The groom is coming!" Her new mother handed her a fresh white bedsheet and said softly, "You can change it afterward."

After? The word echoed like a bell in her mind.

And suddenly, the spell broke.

Panic flooded her chest. *What will happen tomorrow when they check for the signs of virginity on that sheet?*

She trembled. Her breath quickened.

I lost my virginity long ago. I'm already pregnant.

Her hands were cold. Could she tell her husband? *No. He'll kill me.* Or worse, expose her. Shame her. Ruin her mother. *Ruin everything.*

The door closed behind her with a soft, final click.

Hashmat entered the room.

Rani wrapped herself tighter in the ornate fabric around her, like a flower folding itself before a storm. She sat still, heart pounding.

Hashmat approached gently.

"May I?" he asked, kneeling beside her. "Am I allowed to see the queen of my heart?"

He slowly lifted her veil.

She kept her eyes lowered. But then he smiled and placed a small box in her hands. She opened it.

A beautiful gold ring with a sparkling diamond.

She smiled faintly and whispered, "Thank you."

Hashmat's voice was low, almost nervous. "I just want to say… I've never been with a woman in my life."

He looked at her, vulnerable in a way she hadn't expected. "I don't know anything about… this. I've only used my hands for pleasure," he confessed, embarrassed.

Rani's heartbeat slowed.

She had prepared herself for violence, judgment, or coldness. But instead, she found gentleness. Innocence.

In that moment, she prayed.

God… I have never prayed before, not really. But if You are there, if You are who they say you are… then help me. Because this… this I cannot fix on my own.

Hashmat continued speaking softly, his voice tender in the dim light.

"You'll have complete freedom here," he said. "You just need to speak with my mother before making any major decisions in the house. Give her respect, and she'll give you everything, whatever you ask."

He smiled gently. "And my sister, Bisma... she's kind and educated. Live with her like you lived with your own sister."

Then he reached over and turned off the light.

The room went still, but Rani could feel the warm breeze of his breath near her cheek. It stirred something inside her, not desire, but anticipation... and fear.

Outside, in her mind, the waves of an imaginary sea began to rise, mad with energy. They rushed to the shore, crashing against stones, pulling at sand, dancing violently under the invisible pull of a full moon. It was as if nature itself had become restless. Uncertain.

In that imagined sea, a small fish floated quietly. Still. Food lay nearby, fragrant, tempting, warm, but the fish did not move. It was not hunger that filled it, but hesitation. It had no wish to grow. It did not feel the lust to feed. It only hovered.

The piece of meat shimmered under the water like an invitation, but the fish approached it... and instead of biting, it turned and vomited over it, leaving the offering untouched.

The sea calmed. The breeze from Hashmat's mouth ceased.

He turned to the side, silent for a moment.

Then, in a voice tinged with shame, he said, "I'm sorry... I don't know what happened."

Rani looked at him in the dark. The moment had passed, leaving only silence and a bed sheet between them. Her fingers ran across the fabric her mother-in-law had left behind for the morning.

"The bed sheet..." she whispered. "What will I show her in the morning?"

"Oh God," said Hashmat, panic rising. "What do we do now?"

"You're the man," said Rani calmly. "You should decide what to do."

She paused, then added, "And you know it's not my fault."

Hashmat's silence was heavy, trembling.

Rani sat up slightly, her voice firm but kind. "Alright. I'll help you."

He turned to her, confused.

"But promise me," she continued, "that tomorrow, and every time you speak to your friends, you will say I was a virgin. That there was blood. That I cried all night. That in the morning I couldn't walk because… because you were so violent."

Hashmat blinked. Then nodded quickly. "Yes, yes, I will. I'll say exactly that."

Relief poured into Rani's chest like a cool stream. Her secret was safe now.

Her problem *that* problem, was solved.

She had a husband who would never question her again. A man who would never challenge her freedom. A man who needed her more than she needed him.

She smiled in the dark and leaned over, kissing his forehead gently. "You're the best husband," she whispered.

And Hashmat, overwhelmed with gratitude, smiled too. For in this strange dance of truths and lies, shame and acceptance, they had found something rare:

A bond not built on desire, but on unspoken understanding.

Rani, in her quiet strength, took the dead fish in her hands. The one that had floated silently in the stormy sea of her thoughts. She gently placed it within the offering, inside the piece of meat meant for a feast, and brought it back to life. Not in spirit, but in purpose.

For the rest of the night, the fish played its role.

She knew what needed to be done. She knew how to draw a line of blood with the smallest of injuries, enough to mark the sheet, enough to preserve the illusion. She had learned to survive in a world that demanded performance.

Hashmat, relieved, believed the fish had dipped into the meal. That it had eaten. Even if it was once lifeless, it had come to life *for him*.

Later, when the fish returned and quietly vomited within the food, there was no complaint. No judgment.

And Rani smiled.

She smiled because the performance had been completed. The evidence would be there in the morning. The story would be told the way it needed to be. The fish, the food, the blood, the silence, all would work in her favor.

In this quiet act of cooperation, both Hashmat and the fish, his impotence and her secret, had aligned to protect her.

She was safe.

And she had mastered, once again, the art of survival.

The bed sheet was quietly changed in the night and placed among the laundry for the servants to collect. No one came to inspect it. No questions were asked. In this house, a fresh sheet meant the story had been told blood was assumed, honor intact.

Rani continued living with Hashmat, and something unexpected began to happen.

Within a few days, Hashmat changed. Her presence, her softness, her confidence, they worked like slow, healing medicine.

He, who had once trembled in silence and shame, now came to life. The dead fish had learned to swim.

He was no longer impotent.

It's rightly said, *it is a woman who makes a man a real man.* Society rarely understands this truth that many young men labeled "impotent" are only inexperienced, frightened, unsure. Often, it is not their body that betrays them, but their mind.

Intimacy, safety, and mutual care are all more powerful than any medicine. Love is not just a feeling; it's a key. And Rani had unlocked something within him.

Soon, Rani announced her pregnancy. The household erupted in celebration. Hashmat, glowing with pride, believed it was his doing. His manhood affirmed, his heart opened fully to the woman he now saw as a divine gift.

"She is a blessing from God," he said to anyone who would listen. "She made me whole. She made me a man. And now, she will make me a father."

Rani smiled, gently. She had given Hashmat everything he needed to believe. But in her heart, she knew the truth.

The child she carried was not his.

It was Payja's.

Her first and last love.

Though she now belonged to another house, her ties to Payja hadn't vanished completely. Each time she went to his village, supposedly for shopping, she would stop by his shop. The same staircase. The same upper room.

The same silence.

Then came the birth of a son. And from the first moment, anyone who had ever known Payja could see it. The child bore his features like a quiet mirror. The eyes, the nose, the shape of the mouth—it was all there.

But Hashmat, who had never met Payja, saw only joy. The only thing that puzzled him was that the child had arrived slightly early. "It could be dangerous for the baby," he worried aloud.

Rani feigned concern. "Yes, but he's strong. He's survived."

And so, the child celebrated. He was named, kissed, held. Hashmat adored him. Even Payja, who had guessed the truth in silence, would sometimes hold the boy when Rani visited, planting gentle kisses on his hair, never saying a word. He knew he could never claim him.

Time, like a slow current, changed things further.

With her child thriving and Hashmat growing into a confident man, Rani began to change too. Her resistance softened. Hashmat no longer needed guidance he had become a tireless rider. Their nights, once uncertain, turned into routine. Then routine became pleasure. Then... pleasure turned to desire.

She began to enjoy it.

To need it.

To feel something close to love.

The past faded like an old season. Her visits to Payja became less frequent. Months passed between them. And even when she did stop by, it was no longer for touch or intimacy. Something had shifted in her.

She had moved on.

Her life was now filled with money, a child, a man who worshipped her, and the rhythm of a rich household. Her needs had changed.

As for Payja he remained in his shop, quiet, watchful. He would smile at the boy, kiss him gently when Rani allowed it, and then watch her leave again, knowing he had given life to something he could never claim.

The boy bore his blood. But bore another man's name.

And that… was the price.

Chapter 8

THE NEW WORLD

Daniel arrived in the city with a single goal in his heart: to get a visa to India. His journey, long imagined in fireside discussions and whispered in ancient stories, was finally beginning. All he needed now was permission.

He reached the Indian Embassy early in the day, filled with cautious optimism. But what he saw there took the breath out of him.

A line. Not just long but endless. A river of people already coiled outside the gates like pilgrims waiting at a shrine. Some sat on blankets. Some stood, tired. Some camped overnight.

He walked up to a man in the queue. "How long have you been here?" Daniel asked.

The man looked at him, half-smiling. "Since 3 a.m. But even then, many were already ahead. If you want to get inside, you must come the night before or sleep here. That's the only way."

There were no online appointments in those days. No digital forms. Especially not for someone from a village, where the internet was still a distant rumor. Everything had to be done in person, on paper, by patience.

Daniel spent the day at a friend's house in the city. That night, the two of them walked back to the embassy. It was dark, the streets half-silent, but when they reached the embassy gates, others were already there, some wrapped in shawls, others sitting in silence. They joined the silent group, sat for a while, then eventually fell asleep under the open sky.

Before dawn, someone nudged them awake.

"Are you here to sleep or to apply for a visa?" the voice said, half-joking.

Daniel sat up, startled. The line had already formed. He and his friend had slipped further back than they expected but they stayed.

The sun rose. Time crawled. Faces changed in line. Water was passed from stranger to stranger. Finally, after an entire day of waiting, Daniel's friend left for home. Daniel stepped inside the embassy alone.

He had come prepared, form filled, photograph attached, documents in order. He handed the papers to the officer at the window.

"What's the purpose of your visit to India?" the officer asked, barely glancing up.

"I want to travel from the Himalayas to Kanyakumari," Daniel replied.

The officer raised an eyebrow, a hint of a smile playing at the edge of his mouth. "That's quite a journey. Why all these places?"

"I'm looking for herbs," Daniel said calmly. "And I hope to meet some saints."

The officer studied him for a second, as if trying to decide whether this was truth or madness. Then he smiled again. "Alright. Come back next week, same window. You can collect your passport at 11 a.m."

"Do I need to wait in line again?" Daniel asked nervously.

"No," the officer replied. "Pickups are quick. You'll walk straight in."

Daniel stepped out of the embassy, holding the receipt tightly in his hand. The air felt lighter. The traffic noise didn't bother him. His feet ached; his eyes burned, but his heart was flying.

Next week, he will have the visa.

Next week, he will begin.

And India, mystic, chaotic, infinite, would open its arms to him.

Daniel spent the week in the city, staying with his friend Mirza. Islamabad was unlike any other place he had known, clean, quiet, modern. Yet, there were still trees everywhere, and at night, fireflies floated in the dark like sparks from forgotten stars.

One night, Daniel decided to go out to the market in Rawalpindi. He took a taxi, watching the city drift like a dream half awake.

As they drove, the taxi driver suddenly asked, "Do you have your ID card with you?"

Daniel checked his pocket. "No. I left it at home. Why do I need it?"

"You're in Islamabad, brother," the driver said, slowing the car slightly. "The police here don't need a reason. If you don't have ID, they'll stop you, question you... and probably ask for money."

Daniel laughed lightly. "Come on, I'm not a foreigner. I'm speaking Urdu and Punjabi. Do I look like a stranger?"

The driver shook his head. "You still don't understand this place. They don't care how you speak. They just need an excuse."

As if summoned by the very words, the taxi slowed down near a checkpoint.

A uniformed officer stepped forward. "Where are you coming from? Where are you headed?"

"From G-8 to Pir Wadhai," the driver replied, handing over his documents.

The officer nodded, then looked through the window at Daniel. "Your ID?"

"I have it at home," Daniel said calmly.

The officer narrowed his eyes. "That's not how this works. How do I know you're Pakistani? You could be Afghan. Or worse."

Daniel raised his voice slightly, switching into heavy Punjabi. "Do I *look* like I came from another country?"

The officer scowled. "Alright. Let's make it simple, give and take. You give, we let you take the ride."

Daniel stared at him. "You mean… a bribe?"

The officer's face hardened. "You want to play smart?"

Without waiting for a reply, he pulled open the door, yanked Daniel out of the car, and threw him into the back of a police van.

They drove to the local station. There, Daniel was told to sit on the floor—no chair, no dignity. He sat in silence for over an hour.

Finally, a senior officer arrived. "What's going on?" he asked, pointing at Daniel.

"He doesn't have ID," said the constable.

The inspector turned to Daniel. "Why don't you have your card? Are you Afghan?"

Daniel, burning with humiliation, replied, "Do you want me to abuse you in Punjabi, so you believe I'm from Punjab?"

The inspector's face darkened. "Lay him down! Let's show him how we deal with arrogant men!"

But Daniel, seeing how quickly the fire could spread in that place, softened his tone.

"Sir, forgive me. I didn't mean any disrespect. I just didn't have money for your officer. He asked for a bribe… and I refused."

There was a pause.

Then the inspector exhaled, his rage slowly draining. "Don't go out without your ID at night in this city," he said finally. Then he looked at his officer. "It's enough. Let him go."

Daniel stepped outside the station, the night air cooler than he remembered. It was past midnight. He walked home slowly.

His first time in a police station.

And a lesson learned: **the system doesn't want truth. It wants time, power, or money. And if you have none of those it wants your silence.**

After a week, Daniel returned to the Indian Embassy with a beating heart and hope rising in his chest. He stood at the collection window, received the sealed envelope, and stepped aside.

His hands trembled slightly as he opened the envelope, imagining the glossy page of his passport stamped with the beginning of his great journey.

But inside… there was no visa.

Just plain white paper.

A line of text printed coldly across the top: *"Visa denied."*

And beneath it, the reason: *"Purpose of visit unclear."*

For a moment, he couldn't breathe. His dreams shattered not like glass, but like silence breaking in the middle of a prayer.

How could they not give me a visa? he thought. *India…?*

He stepped out onto the road. The embassy behind him now felt like a wall, not a doorway.

We were one country, he thought bitterly. *We speak the same language, eat the same food, tell the same stories, cry the same tears. Our blood is shared by our ancestors who walked the same earth. But still, we are enemies.*

Neighbors, he thought, *who've forgotten how to knock on each other's doors.*

It's okay to fight sometimes but to stop talking all together. To close all doors to the public? That's not war. That's punishment.

He looked up at the sky. It had no borders. No colors. Just open air.

There are no other countries in the world where neighbors deny visas to neighbors, he thought. *Even bitter rivals allow people to pass. But here, we've turned our memories into weapons and sealed them in vaults.*

If people can't visit each other, the distance will grow thicker. The silence becomes deeper. The wounds never close. Only people can bring peace, not governments, not armies. Only people.

He remembered reading once about Europe. How borders had opened. How people traveled, worked, lived freely across countries. *And they still flourish. Still grow. Imagine if we did the same…*

Kashmir would no longer be a point of tension, he thought. *If trade were free, if jobs were open, if people could walk across borders as brothers, there would be no room left for hatred. Hatred lives in isolation. It feeds on fences. We never needed war. We never had a real reason to fight.*

This divide... it was manufactured. Designed. Profitable for some.

Daniel stared down at the paper in his hand.

Now what? he wondered.

How do I get to India now?

They sat in silence.

Daniel. Payja. Rana. Pa Shida.

The room felt smaller than usual. The air heavy with the weight of Daniel's visa rejection. The fire crackled faintly, but no one spoke at first. They simply stared into the flames, thinking.

"What now?" murmured Pa Shida.

"The purpose is too great," said Daniel at last. "We can't just stop here."

Payja leaned back against the wall. "Remember what the saint said? He could travel anywhere without a visa. He *knew* the ways."

"That was then," Daniel replied. "Now it's different. Borders are strict. Fences are real. Satellites see everything."

"But our boys go all the time to fight in Kashmir," Kala chimed in suddenly. "They cross the border like wind."

"Yes," said Daniel, "they go as *Mujahideen*. Fighters. They're trained. Armed. Supported."

"And we're just..." He paused, smiling faintly. "Sanyasis. Smokers. Dreamers."

"You could go like them," Kala said, eyes brightening. "They'll take you in, thinking you're one of them. Once you're in, you slip away. Quietly. And go where we need."

Daniel shook his head immediately. "No chance. I'm not crossing illegally. Especially not into India. It's the most dangerous country for a Pakistani to enter without a visa. You know what would happen if I'm caught?"

Everyone fell silent again.

Then Kala spoke, softly but with a strange confidence, "If you all agree… I'll go."

There was a pause. Then laughter exploded in the room.

"You?" said Pa Shida, shaking his head. "You can't find your own house after one cigarette. And you want to go to India as a Mujahid?"

"Do I look like a fighter to you?" Payja added, wiping tears of laughter.

Even Daniel smiled, despite being himself.

But Kala wasn't joking.

"I can do it," he said. "I'll go through their route. When I'm in India, I'll disappear. I'll follow the saint's path straight to the mountains."

Daniel leaned forward slowly. "Actually… he's right. That route leads exactly where we wanted to start, where the saint first went. It could work."

Everyone looked at each other. The laughter faded. The fire crackled louder now, like it was listening.

"Let him go," Payja said, finally. "If Kala can cross… he'll do what none of us can."

Rana nodded. "Agreed."

Pa Shida rubbed his hands together. "Then it's decided."

And in that quiet room filled with smoke, old secrets, and stubborn dreams, four friends decided to send a hashish-smoking mystic across a deadly border.

Not as a soldier.

Not as a spy.

But as a *Sanyasi* searching for the divine, chasing the formula, and walking in the footsteps of a forgotten saint.

Kala had spoken to his friends in Lashkar-e-Taiba with a strange new courage burning in his chest. "I want to go to Kashmir with you," he said.

The men welcomed him warmly, clapping him on the back. "We always knew," one of them said with pride, "that God would choose you for a greater purpose."

"Yes," another added, "you have been chosen to help free our Kashmiri brothers and sisters. You're no longer just Kala; you're part of the divine cause."

Shy, but carried by the weight of the moment, Kala lifted his chin and spoke. "We will remind the enemy whose land this truly is. And we will throw them out of Jannat-e-Kashmir. His voice trembled with emotion as the others nodded in solemn agreement.

The very next day, he was taken to a hidden camp high in the mountains far away from cities, beyond the reach of familiar life. From the outside, it looked abandoned: mud houses, empty yards, no sign of life.

But as soon as they stepped inside one of the homes, Kala saw it, rows upon rows of young men sleeping, tightly packed into small rooms. Most of them barely moved their faces sunken with fatigue.

It was daytime, but the lights were dim. This week was *night combat training*.

Kala was fed well, better than he expected. A clean mattress was laid out for him. On the wall beside him hung a green commando-style uniform. The camp commander appeared suddenly and barked in a sharp voice, "Ready at 10 p.m. Outside. Full gear."

Kala gave a hesitant nod.

He was surprised at how well-equipped the mud homes were fridges, a functioning kitchen, fresh fruits, milk, and a solid bathroom with running water. There was electricity, and even a sealed-off entrance at the back hidden, secure.

He managed a few hours of uneasy sleep, then woke after nine, took a cold shower, and dressed in the uniform provided. By ten o clock, he stood outside under the cold stars, blending into the crowd of new recruits.

That night there was a blur of running, commands, and exhaustion.

They were handed heavy bags and wooden mock rifles. When the whistle blew, they dropped to the ground. When a shout came, they fired into the darkness, imaginary bullets, real discipline. "Sit!" they sat. "Down!" they dropped flat. They lifted guns and aimed, again and again.

By morning, Kala couldn't move.

His body screamed for rest. He stumbled to the edge of the training yard and collapsed onto a stone bench, panting.

"I'm… I'm finished," he whispered to the recruit next to him. "I can't feel my legs."

The commander approached. "You smoke hashish?" he asked bluntly.

Kala, half-conscious, nodded. "I used to. My friends told me to stop. I'm here for a purpose now."

"Who told you that hashish is forbidden?" the commander snapped. "We don't forbid anything. You think a real fighter wins battles clean? We train with pain. And when the real time comes, we fight with no sleep, no food, no fear. Drugs make that possible."

Kala blinked, confused.

The commander offered him a hand. "Come. You need rest. Let us show you how our soldiers recover."

The commander walked over, his boots crunching lightly on the gravel. His sharp eyes landed on Kala, who was slumped against the side of the training yard, drenched in sweat, barely able to keep his head up.

"Do you smoke hashish?" he asked, flatly.

Kala, still catching his breath, replied, "I used to. But I've come here for a greater purpose. My friends told me to stop."

The commander laughed softly, but not kindly. "Who told you that hashish is forbidden?"

Kala looked up, confused.

"You think you can fight without it?" the commander continued. "You think purity wins wars? No, brother. We use everything. Drugs are tools, like bullets. When the time comes, we'll need to stay awake for days. We'll need to kill without hesitation. That kind of cruelty... that kind of strength doesn't come from prayer alone."

His voice was calm, too calm.

"You must be strong enough *for* the drugs," he said. "That's what makes a real Mujahid."

Then he reached out and took Kala by the hand, lifting him gently. "Come. You're new here. You've earned some rest."

With a subtle signal of his fingers, he gestured to a man standing quietly in the corner. "Today we welcome our new guest," the commander said, smiling. "Take him. Let him recover properly. Treat him well."

Kala followed without speaking, his legs moving more from obedience than will. Something in his chest felt tight not from the night's exhaustion, but from the weight of something far more unsettling.

He had come here believing he was walking a path of sacrifice and honor.

But now, something else was beginning to show beneath the surface, shadow he hadn't expected.

The commander took Kala by the hand and led him quietly through a narrow hallway. They stopped at a heavy wooden door, its edges sealed and guarded. The commander raised two fingers, signaling a nearby attendant.

"Today, we welcome our new guest," he said. "Let him rest. Treat him well."

The attendant nodded and gestured for Kala to follow. They passed through the sealed door, stepping into a part of the compound Kala hadn't seen before, one that seemed worlds apart from the mud walls and training grounds.

Inside, it was warm, dimly lit, and surprisingly modern. Kala paused at the threshold, stunned.

There were women here. Dozens of them. Some sat on plush cushions, laughing softly at a movie playing in the corner. Others lounged in separate rooms visible through arched doorways. Their clothing was loose, revealing, and far from what Kala had expected in a place built on the language of religion and sacrifice.

The attendant smiled as if offering a gift. "You may choose one. Or two. As many as you like."

Kala hesitated, confused. "Is this… allowed?"

The man laughed gently. "This is Jihad. And Mujahid has every right. These women are not what you think. They are here for the cause. Just like you. It's not a sin. It's service."

Kala said nothing.

Everything inside him was beginning to spin. The beliefs he had clung to… the purity he thought he was walking toward… suddenly it all felt like sand slipping between his fingers.

Still, the promise of comfort, of acceptance, was tempting. His body ached. His mind was numb. His soul, confused.

He followed the attendant deeper into the chamber.

He told himself it was part of the process. That this too was preparation.

But something inside him whispered, *this is not what you came here for, but he has to do in Rome as Romans Do.*

Kala entered the room with two women by his side, women who moved with confidence, speaking without hesitation, without shame. They looked at him directly, asked him what he liked, how he wanted to be pleased, what would satisfy him most.

Their ease unsettled him.

Not because they were forward but because they were *certain.* Certain that this was all normal. Expected. Deserved.

Kala had no words. He simply watched them, stunned, his mind trying to catch up to what his eyes were seeing.

This was not the purity he had imagined. This was not the austere world of sacrifice and righteousness he had thought he was joining.

But still… it was seductive. There was warmth here. Comfort. Attention. Luxury. There was no preaching, no pressure, just pleasure. And it welcomed him like a long-lost friend.

Hashish passed around like it was holy. Bottles of alcohol stood uncorked on small tables. Laughter, soft music, silk sheets, it felt less like a battlefield and more like a dream.

So, this is the promised heaven, he thought.

The one they spoke of with shining eyes and trembling voices.

He had imagined it in the clouds, after death, among angels. But here it was — offered in advance. All the desires of the flesh. All the fantasies of power. No guilt. No shame.

And all in the name of Jihad.

He let himself fall into it, not out of belief, but confusion. A part of him still whispered that something wasn't right.

But for now, that voice was small.

And the silence around him was loud.

Almost a month has passed in the mountains.

Day by day, Kala was shaped into someone new. The relentless training, running through the darkness, crawling through mud, firing at silhouettes with deadly precision, turned his body into a weapon. He learned to hold and shoot rifles, to dismantle and reload in seconds, to aim with frightening accuracy.

By the end of four weeks, he had the instincts of a soldier.

And it showed.

The excess fat melted away under the mountain air and discipline. His limbs grew lean, his muscles defined. His movements became swift, his eyes alert. Even though his posture had changed, he stood taller now, carried differently, with the silent pride of someone who had endured and come out the other side.

But it wasn't just the training.

In the hours between drills, there was indulgence. Soft beds. Rich meals. Fruit, milk, warm bread, and heavy meats. There were women too, always available, always smiling. Intimacy was not whispered here. It was routine. Reward. A part of the system.

Between the fight and the feast, Kala had transformed.

He looked at himself in the mirror one morning at a rare moment of stillness. The face that stared back was no longer the one that had sat beside Payja, rolling hashish on the riverbank, laughing under the sun.

This face was sharper. Harder. Framed by shadow.

A handsome, trained *Mujahid.*

Ready for war

Yet, somewhere behind the clear skin and strong shoulders, a quiet question stirred.

Is this what I came for?

But it passed quickly. Training was about to begin.

Chapter 9

DIFFERENT DIRECTIONS

Daniel's fields had become a graveyard of lost hope.

Year after year, the floods came like unwanted guests. The river near his land overflowed with vengeance, drowning his crops in muddy silence. The water stayed for months, leaving the soil too wet, too wounded to grow anything again until the next season.

One crop a year if the sky was merciful.

Summer brought nothing. Not even fodder for the cattle. His cows, once proud and strong, stood dry and silent now. No milk. No grain. Only the weight of loan and the burden of failure pressed down on Daniel's shoulders like the monsoon clouds that had taken everything from him.

He could no longer afford to stay in the village laughing with Payja, dreaming under trees, calling himself a *Sanyasi*.

He needed to move. To survive.

So, he did what many before he had done. He left.

The foreign land felt like another planet. Clean streets. Silent buses. Polite strangers. The buildings stood tall and modern, the air was cold and crisp, and even the sunlight felt different, like it came through a cleaner sky.

The language was strange. The food was unfamiliar. The people didn't look like him. But they were kind. And when you walk with desperation in your heart, the world makes room.

One day, while walking in the city with no real plan, he met a man, Mr. Saeed.

He wore simple clothes, moved with purpose, and had the easy confidence of someone who had lived far from home for many years. When Daniel asked him for help, Saeed studied him for a moment and then smiled.

"Of course," he said. "Come with me."

Saeed had been in Sweden for over twenty years. He owned a cleaning company and employed several people from back home. He was known for his hard work and for being a little unusual.

They walked through quiet streets until they reached a building with a dull, nondescript door. It didn't look like much from the outside, but inside, Daniel saw something different.

Three rooms: one filled with brooms, mops, and cleaning machines. One is set up like a small office desk, computer, calendar on the wall. And one that looked like a living room, with a worn-out sofa, a few scattered chairs, and a tiny kitchen tucked into a corner.

Saeed threw his bag on the sofa and sat down.

"Welcome home," he said with a grin. "This is our office. But we use it for fun too. You'll see soon, many people will come."

Daniel looked around. It wasn't luxury. But it was safe. Warm. Real.

And most importantly, it was the beginning.

"Now," said Saeed, leaning back in his chair, his tired eyes studying Daniel with quiet curiosity. "Tell me your story."

Daniel sighed, the weight of it was still heavy in his chest. "I came here because I had no choice. Back in Pakistan, our fields are ruined by floods every year. The water comes, drowns everything, and stays for months. You can't grow food. Not even for the cattle. Loans piled up. Life became… impossible. Bread and butter weren't just hard to earn. It felt like a distant dream."

He paused, then continued. "When I got here, I called my relative. He had invited me once; said he would help if I ever came. But he didn't answer my calls. I tried asking other countrymen in the streets, at shops but no one helped. Then I met you. You listened. You said yes. And here we are."

Saeed gave a thoughtful nod. Then he turned to the computer and cracked his fingers like a man ready to play a game he'd already won. "What's your relative's name?"

"Rashid Ali."

"Age?"

"Maybe in his forties?"

"Hm." Saeed typed with quick, confident fingers. "In Sweden, everyone can be found. Home address, registration — everything is public. It's called the right to information."

A few seconds passed. Saeed squinted, then smirked.

"Here he is," he said, turning the screen slightly toward Daniel. "Lives nearby. And guess what?"

"What?"

"He's living with an old woman."

Daniel frowned. "That can't be. He once showed me a photo; his wife was young. Very beautiful."

Saeed chuckled as he peeled off his socks, the smell wafting through the small office like another reminder of life's raw truths.

"You'll learn, Daniel. Give it a few days. In this country, nothing is what it looks like."

He tossed the socks aside, leaned back with a grin, and added, "Most of the men from India and Pakistan, what do they do? They find an old woman, marry her, and get their residence permit. That's the shortcut. It's not love. It's survival."

Daniel sat quietly, unsure whether to feel disappointed, amused, or just more awake.

And so, the curtain slowly began to lift on a life he thought he understood but hadn't even begun to see.

"For now," Saeed said as he grabbed his coat, "I want to show you something."

They stood in the narrow hallway of the office. Saeed looked Daniel in the eyes, serious now. "But before we go, listen to me carefully: no fighting, no accusing. If he says no—walk away. Don't tell him how we met. Just see for yourself. And if you still need help, come back here. I'll be around."

Daniel nodded.

Saeed handed him the car keys. "You drive."

Daniel blinked. "Me?"

"Yes, you. It's time."

Daniel took the keys and slipped behind the wheel. The steering was on the left, the opposite to what he was used to. In Pakistan, he had driven countless roads. Here, the lanes ran the other way. But his hands were steady. He adjusted quickly.

Saeed navigated using his phone. The roads were clean, the signs quiet. No horns, no chaos, just cold order and sharp turns.

They stopped in front of a modest apartment building tucked between bare trees. The grey sky hung low. Saeed stepped out, glanced at the row of post boxes by the entrance, and ran a finger down the labels.

"Here. Second floor."

They climbed the stairs.

Daniel's heart beat heavier with each step.

Saeed knocked.

The door opened. A large, older woman stood there, wearing a loosely tied robe. She spoke in Swedish; Daniel didn't understand a word. But he caught one name as Saeed replied calmly: "Rashid Ali."

The woman's tone softened. She smiled faintly. "Husband," she said, pointing back into the apartment. "Gone to the market for wine. He's coming soon."

And just like that, she shut the door.

They returned to the parking lot. Saeed hid behind a pillar, leaving Daniel alone to face what would come.

Minutes passed.

Then Rashid appeared, two bottles of wine in his hands, his coat open to the chill wind. He froze when he saw Daniel.

He said, "Daniel?" his eyes wide. "How did you… how are you here?"

Daniel stood straight. "In Sweden, everyone can be found," he said quietly.

Rashid's face lost its color.

"Did you knock on my door?" he asked.

"Yes," Daniel replied. "Your wife answered."

Rashid shifted. "She's not my wife. She's… my wife's mother."

Daniel gave a small, tiring smile. "Come on. It's your life. You don't need to explain."

There was a pause. Then Daniel asked, gently, "Do you have a place for me? Or should I go stay with someone else?"

Rashid looked down, ashamed. "It's better you go. If you have someone else. She's strict. I must stay quiet for at least one more year until I get my permanent residence."

Daniel nodded.

"You could've just told me, "He said. "You could've answered the phone. I would've understood. But instead, you ignored me. Left me wandering around in a city I didn't know. That wasn't right."

Rashid said nothing.

Daniel stepped back. "It's okay. Thank you. Goodbye."

And he walked to the car.

Rashid stood still for a few seconds. Then he turned, slowly, and climbed the stairs, back to his temporary home, his silent compromises, and his deal with time.

They drove in silence for a while, the glow of streetlights slipping over the windshield like calm waves. Then Saeed spoke, his voice gentle, reflective.

"You know, Daniel… when I first saw you standing there, asking for help, I saw myself. That was me, twenty years ago."

Daniel glanced at him, listening closely.

"Not many people ask strangers for help these days. But you did. And I did, once too. When life corners you, you learn that asking just asking can be the bravest thing. Sometimes, when we're drowning, we forget that the person walking by might reach in and pull us out. That's what happened to me. And now, I'm just doing what someone did for me."

Daniel felt a warmth rise in his chest.

Saeed continued, shifting the conversation with a smile. "Now, listen. You can stay here. This office is more than one office. It's a home for many of us."

"I won't lie, we're a business, and things aren't perfect. But we pay 70 crowns per hour to workers without documents. You'll live here, work with us, eat with us, and if you want, laugh with us too."

Daniel nodded. It was more than he could've dreamed.

By the time they reached the building, it was nearly 9 o'clock on a cold Saturday evening. The street was quiet, but inside, the warmth of lights and the smell of distant species made it feel like a hidden corner of home.

Saeed pushed open the door and waved Daniel in.

"Come in. From now on, this place, this is yours too. That sofa there, in the corner, is your bed when you're alone. You'll find blankets inside the cupboard. And the kitchen is yours now, so…"

He clapped his hands together with a grin.

"You're the chef tonight. I'm your guest. Show me what you've got."

Daniel laughed. For the first time in weeks, he felt his shoulders relax. He opened the small fridge, found rice, onions, and a few tomatoes. His hands knew what to do.

As he started to cook, he looked over at Saeed, who had kicked off his shoes and was watching television, humming softly.

He's a saint, Daniel thought. *Maybe even a messenger. A representative of God, sent just for me.*

He had come to a foreign land with no home, no plan, and no name on paper.

And now, in a simple office filled with warmth, spices, and soft light, he had everything he needed.

Late that night, after the meal had been devoured and Daniel's cooking praised with true delight, Saeed leaned back in his chair and grinned.

"You cook like a chef, Daniel," he said. "But now it's time for something different."

Daniel raised a brow. "Where to?"

Saeed only smiled. "Come. I'll show you."

They stepped out into the cold night, climbed into the car, and soon were heading toward the heart of Stockholm. The streets filled with light and energy. Music drifted in waves from street corners and open doors. It was Saturday night, and the city was alive.

They reached a packed street near the center, parked the car, and joined a line outside a dimly lit building. When they reached the front, a man stamped their hands and waved them through.

Inside, there was another world.

Bass thundered beneath their feet. Colored lights danced through thick air. People moved in rhythms, some graceful, some wild. Girls with golden hair laughed into the night. Men in sleek jackets leaned at the bar. Smoke curled in the outside corners. Drinks sparkled in glass.

Daniel blinked, taking it all in. It was like stepping into a dream.

Saeed turned to him, already holding two drinks. "Tonight," he said, raising a glass, "this is heaven. Go, Daniel. Find a girl, talk, laugh, dance. Live. This is your night."

Daniel smiled, wide and childlike, and took the drink.

He walked toward the dance floor and locked eyes with the most beautiful girl in the room, hair like sunlight, lips red as fire. He offered her a drink, and to his surprise, she smiled and accepted. They spoke. They laughed. And then they danced. Under neon lights and loud music, Daniel lost all sense of time.

Saeed, meanwhile, had charmed a woman in her forties, graceful, elegant. They shared a bottle, danced closely, and whispered into each other's ears like old lovers.

Around three in the morning, they stumbled back to the car, warmth still on their cheeks, laughter still hanging in the air.

But before Daniel could start the engine, Saeed raised his hand.

"Give me a moment," he said.

He and the woman stayed in the car, windows fogging, the vehicle gently swaying in place like it was caught in ocean waves.

Daniel waited outside, leaning against the cool night air. The music in his ears had faded now, but the energy of it still echoed in his chest.

Soon, the door opened. Saeed and the woman stepped out, their faces flushed, hair slightly undone, clothes rumpled. The woman kissed Saeed on the cheek and disappeared into the street.

Saeed handed the keys to Daniel. "Drive."

And they went home.

To Saeed, it was just another night.

To Daniel it was the beginning of something he couldn't name yet.

Daniel had finally found what so many seek when they cross oceans and borders: a place to sleep, a way to earn, and the dignity of self-reliance. His job was simple, he was a cleaner.

Nothing glamorous. No titles. No recognition. But it was honest work, and most importantly, it paid.

In a world where undocumented workers were often treated like shadows, paid one-third the going rate, ignored when injured, and discarded without notice, Daniel considered himself lucky. Many of his kind worked long hours without overtime, slept in storerooms, or waited months to be paid. Some were never paid at all.

But Daniel had something rare. He had Saeed.

Saeed, who had once been just a stranger on the street, had become a friend. A guide. A bridge between survival and stability.

Though officially the employer, Saeed treated Daniel like a younger brother. They shared food, shared jokes, and often shared the road because Saeed, for reasons of health and habit, couldn't drive. Daniel became his unofficial chauffeur, navigating the city's quiet streets at dawn and weaving through its neon chaos at night.

Nightlife, too, had become a familiar rhythm.

While others counted their loneliness in hours, Daniel counted streetlights and bar tabs. Stockholm's cold evenings were often softened by music, warmth, and laughter echoing from quiet corners of the city.

No, it wasn't the life he had dreamed of as a boy back home. But it was something.

He had a bed. He had a wage. He had freedom even if it came wrapped in uncertainty.

And sometimes, just sometimes, that was enough.

Chapter 10

CROSSING BORDER

Kala had completed his training.

His body was stronger, his mind shaped by routine and rhetoric, his name now quietly tied to a mission far bigger than himself or so he believed.

He returned to the village briefly, not as a son of the soil, not as an embroidery worker with rough fingers and quiet evenings but as a man ready to cross borders, ready to disappear. It was not India or jihad that stirred him, it was gold. Their dream. The mission. The unspoken belief that, somehow, they would succeed and return as kings.

He came to say goodbye.

To hug his six-year-old daughter one last time. To whisper a lie to his wife.

"I'm leaving," he said softly, his arms around his daughter.

"Where?" she asked, her voice trembling.

"To Kashmir. For jihad."

The lie hit her like lightning. She collapsed to the floor limp, breathless, lifeless.

The screams came next.

Neighbors poured into the house, fanning her with plastic hand fans, rubbing her hands and feet, splashing water on her face. Someone shouted, "Call the doctor!" Others cried out prayers, hoping to pull her back from the edge of this storm.

Minutes passed before she blinked.

"He's going to jihad," she sobbed.

The crowd split in reaction.

Some lifted their hands in prayer, "Mashallah." Others whispered, "He's brave." But a few more quiet, more knowing exchanged glances of concern. He had parents, a wife, and a child. He was needed here, not in the mountains with a rifle in his hand and death in his eyes.

Many men in their village chose jihad not out of ideology, but escape.

When life became unbearable, when loans rose and dignity shrank, when a man could no longer earn bread for his family or respect from his peers, jihad offered a shortcut. It promised honor without the hard work. Glory without the grind. It wrapped cowardice in the robe of sacrifice.

And no one dared to question it.

A man who couldn't face his own poverty could still die like a hero, if he died under a flag.

Kala's friends knew the truth. This wasn't about war or religion. This was about gold. About a dream that they had carved together in silence, bonded by fire, herbs, and impossible hope.

Daniel had promised Kala "I'll send money. Every month. Your daughter will not go hungry."

It was one of the reasons Daniel had gone abroad. To work. To keep the promise. To hold the pieces together while Kala risked everything for the mission.

The village that once echoed with their laughter, the canal where they had stood, naked as brothers in a line, eating cold watermelon like wild dogs fighting for joy, was quiet now.

The sanyasi was scattering.

The boyhood dream had grown teeth. And now, it was biting back.

Kala was leaving. His wife could not stop him.

Finally, he met Payja and Rana. They called Daniel, and Daniel assured him, "Do not worry about your home. I will take care of your family until you are back."

Payja spoke next. "We are here too. We'll all take responsibility."

In the morning, a van came.

Kala departed from his village.

By evening, they were near the border to Indian Kashmir yet still within Azad Kashmir. They stopped at one house. Inside, they were served a nice meal. It was their last meal before crossing over.

The cooks, the men inside, they were all army. Kala could see their uniforms, their ranks. Ten men sat in silence, eating with focus, not joy.

After the food, they were given uniforms. The kind Mujahideen wear. Each was handed a bag. Inside were dry fruits, dates, some drugs, a few injections, and medicine.

Then they were taken to another room.

Here, they were dressed fully, belts, vests, gear. Weapons were issued with guns, bullets, and as many as they could carry. Magazines, grenades. Each man was given one special jacket.

Kala too.

He recognized it from training.

It was a suicide jacket.

He already knew the rules: *When there's no hope for escape, when you're surrounded, you don't surrender. You detonate. Because in Jihad, there is no rule.*

They were told they'd be in Srinagar tomorrow. By 3 a.m.

The army itself let them cross the border. Guided them through. They were given maps.

They walked all night, over mountains and shadows. Silence, except for boots and breath.

By 2 o'clock in the morning, they reached a small road. A tractor trolley loaded with grass was waiting.

They were told to lie down. The grass covered them.

A local Kashmiri farmer drove them quietly toward the city.

One hour later, they were already in Srinagar.

Kala peeked out through the grass.

Daylight was beginning to stretch through the mountains. He could see the shimmer of a lake below, silver and soft. The city is surrounded by peaks. He had arrived. The land looked calm, almost sacred.

By sunrise, they reached a huge cattle farm on the outskirts.

The trolley stopped. They were pulled out from under the grass.

"Here, you will rest till evening," said the commander. "Your mission begins tonight."

They were given milk to drink. And bread. Simple, soft, soaked in milk.

The last comfort before the next darkness.

Now Kala had only one thing in his mind: *How do I escape from this?*

Sometimes he thought, *Maybe I should participate in jihad for now, and if I survive, I can continue my gold mission next.* But he couldn't find any way to escape. All ten Mujahideen were together all the time. They were almost locked inside the farm.

The day passed. Then came the night.

A commander came and stood before them.

"These bloody Indian Hindus should know today how it feels when true Muslims reclaim their land," he said. "Your mission is to blast the airport terminal. Kill anyone you see moving. Do not show pity. Do not spare anyone, armed or unarmed, man, woman, or child. Whoever comes in the way, you shoot."

"Not a single bullet should be wasted. Each bullet should kiss someone's body."

"As soon as you blast the main entrance, you will move toward the parked planes. There should be at least two planes on the runway. Destroy them."

"Army vehicles will be in your path. Security checks too. You must pass through them. Just shoot and kill anyone in the way."

"It's about one kilometer from the checkpoints to the terminal. One kilometer you must survive. Then plant the bombs and blast the terminal. Use grenades to kill the crowd inside."

That was the instruction.

Kala was quiet.

He thought, *why should I shoot even women and children? And people on the airport, won't they be Muslims too? As far as I know, most people in Srinagar are Muslims. Only a few Hindus live here.*

Why should we kill without knowing who we are killing? Muslim or Hindu, innocent or guilty, how can we kill blindly?

These thoughts were capturing Kala's mind like chains.

Only one answer came to him: *When you fight for a cause, many innocent people die too.*

But then another question followed: *What if the cause we are fighting for is false?*

What if we are lied to? What if all these killings and deaths won't bring anything positive at all?

What if this isn't jihad? What if this is just murder?

Kala breathed heavily.

Anyway, he thought, *I will not kill. I will run away.*

They were going in three cars, one leading, the others chasing close behind.

Kala was sitting in the third car with three others. The lead vehicle was running fast toward the airport. Kala saw a board: *Airport 10 kilometers.*

His breath was uneven.

How could I jump out now? he thought. *If I try to escape, my fellow Mujahideen might kill me themselves.*

He felt trapped. No chance to run. No way out.

I have no other option than to complete the mission, thought Kala.

Then, the shots rang out.

Bullets fired from the first car. Smoke rose.

They did not stop.

Kala saw three dead bodies at the first checkpoint.

Then came the second checkpoint.

This time, all three cars were stopped.

Everyone had to kill.

Mujahideen began shooting at anyone they saw. Bodies dropped everywhere on the road, on the sidewalk, between cars.

Three of the Mujahideen were killed in return fire.

Only two cars remained by the time they reached the third checkpoint.

Gunfire continued, aimed at every living human in sight.

Except Kala.

Kala didn't shoot. He couldn't. His purpose was never to kill. He just watched frozen, horrified.

Smoke rose all around. Blasts exploded nearby, clouds of dust and fire swallowing the road. A fuel tank was hit and burst into flames.

At the checkpoint, everyone was dead.

Then Kala saw a bag lying near a fallen soldier. Someone had just returned from leave and had been shot immediately by Mujahid.

Kala rushed to the bag.

Inside were civilian clothes.

He threw off his own uniform, tossed away his weapons, and changed quickly. Now he looked like a regular man. A traveler. Nobody.

He lay down on the ground.

Bullets kept flying.

Then, silence.

Someone shouted, "Kala is missing! Maybe he's been killed!"

"Forget him! Move, move! We need to go!" another voice replied.

The two remaining vehicles rushed toward the terminal.

Two more blasts were heard. Then silence again.

Both vehicles were destroyed by the army. All Mujahideen were killed.

Kala stayed low, heart pounding.

Then he stood up and started walking back toward the city.

Army vehicles passed by.

He looked just like any other civilian now.

Indian and Pakistani, same face, same clothes, same language. No one could tell the difference. He blended in.

He was safe.

But now he had another problem, he had to reach the city. He needed money to take the bus. He had to call Daniel.

But how?

He had no documents, no ID. He couldn't receive any money legally.

What shall I do then? he thought.

He would have to beg. He had no other choice.

He couldn't tell anyone who he was, if someone found out, they could report him to the army. He would be imprisoned. Or worse.

Soon, Kala was in the city again.

He had already made his clothes dirty like beggar's dust all over his body so people would pity him. His beard was long, his face looked worn, like a man who had never taken a shower in his life.

Who should I start begging from? he thought. *And how should I beg? What if people curse me? What if I'm ashamed or thrown away?*

He had no experience begging. But then again, he had no experience in Jihad either.

Now he was a Mujahid, a runaway terrorist in the eyes of India.

But maybe no one even knows how many came as Mujahideen, he thought.

Anyway, he approached a man near a shop and said, "Please help me. I need something to eat."

The man, an old gentleman in nice clothes, looked at him and said, "Why don't you work instead of begging?"

"You can give me work, I can do it," Kala replied. "But right now, I need money to eat. I'm not begging, just asking for help."

"I know you'll just smoke hashish with the money," the man said. "But fine, I'll pay for your food myself. Go sit there in that restaurant, I'll pay them for your meal."

Kala sat on the bench near the restaurant and told the waiter, "That old man will pay for my food. Give me something good to eat."

They gave him Kashmiri mutton with rice. He ate and thanked God for the meal.

Now he had more energy for begging, if needed.

But the old man came again and asked, "Where are you from? If I give you work, can you do it?"

Kala said, "Yes, I can work. But I need money to go back to Delhi."

"Alright," the old man said. "Come with me. We need help on our farm. I'll pay you good money. Work for five days and you'll have enough to reach Delhi."

Now Kala has work.

While Kala lived and worked with the old man on the farm, he had a chance to climb the hills nearby.

He knew the saint had traveled from Kashmir, from Srinagar to Rameshwaram. And somewhere in Srinagar, he had found something important.

Kala remembered.

The herb, *Sanjivani Booti*, also called *Jeewan Booti* was said to glow in the night.

So, Kala began searching under moonlight.

Each night, after the day's labor, he went quietly into the hills. He knew what to look for. He remembered what he had been told.

On the third night, he found it.

A sight like stars glittering across the hillside.

The herb shimmered in the dark, glowing gently, beautifully like fireflies frozen in a dance, or drops of starlight resting on the earth.

His breath caught.

It was real.

He reached out and as soon as he touched the herb, the glow faded.

As if some chemical on the surface, like the powder on a butterfly's wings, had made it shine and vanished with contact.

Still, he knew what it was.

He carefully gathered as much of the herb as was available. Quietly. Gently.

This was it.

His first goal achieved.

He worked as a laborer on the man's farm. The work was hard, but he worked day and night without complaint. The old man gave him food and a place to sleep.

After three days, the old man said, "You're a good man. I thought you were just a beggar. But now I see you're not."

"If you want, you can stay and work here on the farm forever."

Kala replied, "Actually, I lost my bag and my money. That's why I was asking for help when I first met you. But now I really need to go to Delhi."

The old man gave him the money.

Kala took the bus from the station towards Delhi. The road winded through beautiful mountains. The air was fresh. The sky was quiet.

And he, he was finally leaving the life of a ghost behind. In Delhi, Kala had planned to search for the four poisons and the water of the *22 Kunds*. That was his next step.

But how will I return to Pakistan after that? he wondered.

No problem, he told himself. *I'll cross the border the same way I did before.*

The bus was moving steadily when it suddenly stopped at a checkpoint.

Everyone started pulling out their ID cards.

An army man boarded the bus and began checking each ID carefully.

Kala had none.

He thought about running but there was no way. No chance.

"*Aadhar card?*" the officer asked, coming to him.

"I don't have one," replied Kala.

"Where are you going?"

"Delhi," Kala said.

"Without Aadhar card, how did you come from Kashmir? And now heading to Delhi?" the man asked, eyeing him suspiciously.

"Gentleman, I don't have any card," Kala replied. "I'm from Delhi—I came to Kashmir to find some herbs."

He showed them the herbs he had collected.

But they didn't believe him.

He was arrested.

It was a crime to travel without ID in such areas. Or, at the very least, he had to prove his identity.

He was taken to the police station.

"There will be an inquiry," one officer said.

"It can take several days," added another.

"Do you have money?" asked a third.

"No," Kala said quietly. "I don't have any money."

They asked him about his home, his address, his relatives.

Kala couldn't answer clearly. His replies raised more doubt than they cleared.

They began to suspect he was a spy.

Kala was sent to prison.

Chapter 11

SHAHEED KALA

It was early morning. People were enjoying *hukka* at Payja's shop when a van pulled up from the city. Three men stepped out.

"Where is Payja?" one of them asked.

"I'm here, bro," Payja replied, stepping out of the toilet, drying his hands.

"Come, we need to go to Kala's home," said the man.

Payja recognized them immediately they were the same men who had taken Kala for his *Mujahid* training.

"Is everything okay?" he asked, eyeing them carefully.

"Yes, yes... let's talk there," said the man, motioning toward the road.

When they reached Kala's house, his wife ran out the moment she saw the van. Her heart was pounding. She hoped for a letter, a message, some news from her husband.

She brought out chairs and offered them politely. "Please, be seated. I'll make some tea," she said.

"No, please," said the man. "Sit here. No need for tea. First... listen to us."

He looked at her, then around at the gathering crowd. "We have bad news for you," he began. "But first, let us say, Kala made you, and this entire village, proud."

People from the neighborhood began arriving, sensing the news was big. The man stood up on a chair and began to speak, loud enough for all to hear.

"Dear people of this brave and noble village... you'll be proud to know that Kala fought like a tiger for the cause of Kashmir. He sent ten Indian cowards to hell! He completed his mission bravely. The Indian army could not stop him. Five of their military vehicles were destroyed in broad daylight under his fire!"

Cheers erupted in the crowd.

"He captured the front position single-handedly," the man continued. "And then, one bullet came from nowhere, striking him in the chest. But he didn't stop. He kept fighting! Until the very last drop of his blood, he stood firm... and finally, he embraced *Shahadat*, the blessed martyrdom, with the will of Allah Almighty."

People shouted "*Mashallah!*" and chants of "*Takbeer... Allahu Akbar!*" echoed in the street.

Kala's wife burst into tears. She collapsed into her chair, overwhelmed. Their small daughter stood beside her, confused, unable to understand whether she should cry or smile, seeing both grief and pride painted across every face.

Payja stood quietly, frozen in thought.

You bloody idiot... he whispered to himself. *You were supposed to escape and search for the herbs. Not become a soldier.*

While he was lost in his thoughts, the man continued.

"You are our responsibility now," he told Kala's wife. "You will receive monthly support from our organization. Your children will get free education for life."

He reached into his pocket, pulled out an envelope, and handed her a check.

"For now, this is a humble offering, fifty thousand rupees. In honor of your husband's sacrifice."

Kala's wife took the check silently, her hands trembling.

"When will we get his body?" asked Payja.

"We actually don't know yet," the man replied. "Unfortunately, Indians don't return the bodies of the *Mujahideen*. They consider them terrorists."

"But he was your responsibility," said Payja, visibly tense. "We should receive his body, so we can bury him with respect. He's our first *Shaheed*, our first martyr from this small village. We want to build his shrine here."

"For a shrine, you don't need the body," said the man casually. "You can build it without one. There are thousands of shrines in our country without known graves. Many are so old, no one even remembers who's buried there or when they were built."

Payja clenched his fists but said nothing.

These men took our friend... a husband, a father... and they don't even realize what this family has lost. But what did they gain from this? What was the point? he thought.

The whole village gathered at Kala's home after the news spread. People poured in with smiles and praises.

"Do not cry, be proud!" they said to Kala's wife.

"*Shaheeds* are not dead. They are alive, it's written in the Quran!" declared the village *mullah* with a chest full of pride.

"The man who used to smoke *hashish*... who never did anything good in his life," added the *maulana*, "God chose that very man to be the first martyr of our village!"

Kala's wife sat silently, confused. *Were they praising him... or mocking him by recalling his flaws in public?*

Then came Rana.

"We are sorry for your loss," he said gently, "but thankful to God that Kala made us all proud. Please don't cry, be proud. We are with you. From now on, this whole village is your family. You are the daughter of this land, and your child... the child of the entire village."

"Come on," whispered Payja in Rana's ear, "the child is only Kala's."

Kala's wife looked around slowly.

Her eyes scanned the faces. The crowd. The noise. Pride.

But she was searching.

If a shaheed is alive, she thought, *then Kala should be here... somewhere.*

But he wasn't.

And no one could tell her why.

This is one of the most unfortunate truths humanities never dare to confront.

Every human being who has ever been used in war, in the name of freedom, faith, conquest, or revolution has always been used by *someone.* That *someone* could be a king, a government, a private organization, or a religious order. But the fact remains: for centuries, men have been used as tools.

From Alexander the Great to Genghis Khan, from Hitler to the Roman Emperors, from Napoleon to modern-day leaders, men have been taught the same lesson: *if you die for a cause, you are a martyr. A hero. A legend. The world will remember you with pride.*

Society feeds this narrative.

Nations build statues of fallen warriors, placing them in public squares like sacred idols to remind the common man that death for the cause is the highest honor. But what caused it? Most of the time, these causes were fake, manipulated, or built on the thirst for power.

What was Alexander's cause?

What drove Genghis Khan?

What made Hitler believe he had the right to kill millions?

What dream did Napoleon follow as he marched into Russia?

These men used human lives like fuel. Millions were slaughtered. Entire generations erased. But history only remembers the names of the conquerors, not the countless men and women who died under their flags.

What about the families left behind?

The children who never saw their fathers again?

The mothers who never found peace?

The wives who cried into empty beds for decades?

They are forgotten.

Society offered them no tribute. No shrine. No statue. Only slogans.

And today, in Kala's village, the same cycle continues.

People are still being used for Jihad. Still being sent to die for causes they didn't create and don't fully understand. When they die, songs are sung, fake pride is shared, and shallow comfort is offered to the grieving.

But the dead will not return.

They will not eat with their families again.

They will not raise their children.

They will not grow old.

And nothing, *no shrine, no speech, no medal* can bring them back.

This is not new. This is ancient.

And tragically, it will keep happening.

Until one day, we dare to ask:

Who profits from our sacrifice?

And why do we call it honor... when it's only loss?

Payja and the others gathered once more, this time not to laugh, not to scheme but to build.

A shrine.

A monument to Kala.

The whole village had offered prayers for him. His name was on every tongue for days. Children heard his story like a legend. Men spoke of his bravery. Women wept, praised, and whispered. In just a few days, Kala had become something bigger than life.

They built a beautiful shrine in his honor.

At the entrance, carved into polished stone, it read:

"Our great hero, Faiz-ul-Hassan (Kala)"

Most people didn't even know his real name. Only his family knew it.

He had always been Kala "the black one" named for his dark skin when he was born. In villages like theirs, nicknames weren't just names. They were fates. A child with cat-like green eyes would be called *Billa*. If someone couldn't hear well, they were *Bola*. A man with no arms? *Tunda*. Someone slow or confused? *Bonga*.

Cruel names. Casual names. Permanent names.

Kala had carried his name like a second skin.

Now it is engraved in marble.

The inscription praised him as "The great warrior of the village, who fought and gave his life for the honor of our land."

His date and place of death were written beneath it:

Martyred in Srinagar.

Verses from the Qur'an, glorifying the martyr were carved into the stone in delicate Arabic script.

The shrine itself was stunning.

Its walls were lined with cool *marmar* stone, smooth under the touch and cold even in the heat of summer, so visitors could pray in comfort.

A flag stood tall near the headstone. And inside, set neatly on a pedestal, was a glass box with a tiny hole at the top, locked and secure. A donation box. From now on, people would come, offer coins, rupees, whatever they could spare for the upkeep of this sacred space.

Every year, his martyrdom day would be celebrated with *bhandara*, free food for all. *Haleem and naan* would be cooked in giant cauldrons and served to the poor and the faithful.

An oil lamp would burn continuously in the shrine, symbol of light, of presence. People would bring oil to keep it lit, especially on Thursdays, believed to be a holy day.

Threads would be tied to the shrine's iron grilles and walls.

Each thread, a prayer.

A plea.

A girl whose marriage never happened.

A couple who couldn't have a child.

A boy who wanted to top his exams.

A merchant desperate for his business to grow.

They would all come to Kala now.

They would ask him for help.

They would whisper to him like he was listening.

They would believe deeply, truly, that Kala, the martyr, could grant them these things.

But there was one person Kala could not help.

His wife.

And his child.

They would need more than prayers and threads.

They would need food.

Money.

Clothes.

Support.

Kala had left them nothing. No land. No savings. No inheritance. Only a memory. Only a shrine. And so, they would survive on the charity of the village, the same village that now called him *their warrior*.

Kala could not leave behind a roof or a salary.

But he could leave behind a miracle factory.

And so, the miracle business began.

Chapter 12

PERSPECTIVE

Daniel was devastated when he heard about Kala's death.

They had grown up together, played in the same dusty fields, bathed in the same canal, dreamed the same impossible dreams. From childhood until the day he left for another country, Kala had been a part of his every memory. *That's why I told them not to go to India like Mujahideen,* Daniel thought bitterly. *But they didn't listen.*

He continued sending money to Kala's wife every month. By now, his own life had changed. His cleaning job had turned into something bigger. He had grown his own business, and with stability came quiet peace. In a foreign land, surrounded by snow and silence, he had found a kind of order.

In Sweden, he learned, there were only two real ways to meet people, either in a church or at a disco. Daniel didn't enjoy loud places, so he chose the church. He believed the most beautiful souls in Sweden gathered there. People smiled, greeted warmly at the doors, shared stories over *fika*, a cherished Swedish ritual of drinking coffee together after Sunday service. Sometimes, it felt like people went to church just for *fika*. They spent more time in the coffee room than in prayer.

Inside the church, no one judged you. But outside, things shifted.

The same people who hugged you after service might not even greet you on the street the next day. You might wave, say hello and get nothing but a polite nod before they turn away. Daniel found this strange. In his home country, when you shared food or tea, you became friends for life. But each culture had its own code.

In India and Pakistan, people worshipped white skin. A European living there was treated like royalty. But in Europe, it wasn't the same for South Asians. Racism was quiet but present. A white man in Karachi could marry easily. But a Pakistani man in Sweden? Rarely would a white woman accept him as a husband.

Daniel had come to understand that living in Europe meant something deeper than just being physically present. If you didn't adopt the values, the lifestyle, the rhythm of this society, your heart would always feel misplaced. Many immigrants lived in parallel societies, clustering in neighborhoods by origin. Somalis lived among Somalis, Syrians with Syrians, and so on. They recreated the life they left behind.

And the locals? They didn't like it.

At work, Daniel saw things that puzzled him. People washing their feet in the same basins used for hands. Toilets left wet after someone washed in ways unfamiliar to Swedes. *Why do they do this here?* He wondered. *Why can't they adapt to the country they live in?*

Daniel wasn't judging. He had simply changed. He now believed that if one wanted to live in Sweden, then they should live *like Swedes*. Otherwise, what was the point? If one wanted Islamic schools and Sharia law, then why not move to Saudi Arabia or the Gulf? These were questions he never dared to speak aloud, but they burned within him.

Eventually, Daniel became a stranger to his own community. They said he had grown *too proud*. But it wasn't pride, it was adaptation. He had learned to love this land. Built a new family. Learned the value of freedom, privacy, simplicity.

Still, he never forgot his old promises.

He kept sending money to Kala's family.

Every now and then, Payja and Rana would call him. *"Come, Daniel. Fly to India. Finish what Kala couldn't."*

But he was afraid.

"It's your turn now," said Payja firmly, staring into the screen during a late-night video call.

Daniel smiled faintly, rubbing his temples. "My dear, so many years have passed... let's forget about that now."

"No," Payja snapped. "It won't end like that. One of our friends, Kala, sacrificed his life for the cause of our mission. For the gold. And now, just because you have a comfortable life in Sweden, you want to pretend it never mattered?"

Daniel stayed silent, the image of Kala's laughing face flickering in his mind like a dying candle.

"Don't forget," Payja continued, his voice softening. "Why are we all separated. Why Kala went to India. Why *you* went to Sweden. It wasn't just for survival but for the dream we all shared. We were *sanyasis*, remember?"

Daniel looked away for a moment. The silence on the call was louder than the ticking of the wall clock in his room.

Finally, he spoke. "Alright. I'll try to get an Indian visa from here."

A smile slowly crept onto Payja's face. "Now that's my brother."

Daniel nodded, knowing he had just agreed to reopen a chapter of his life he thought was long closed.

But now, as a Swedish citizen, traveling to India was much easier than it had ever been before. Easier than it had been for Kala. Easier than it would have been as a Pakistani.

And maybe... just maybe... it was time.

While living in Sweden, Daniel had immersed himself in countless books. He studied nearly every major religion, compared cultures, observed habits, and absorbed the perspectives of different nations through the lens of a multicultural society. Over the years, he has transformed. He was no longer the man who once arrived, young and uncertain, chasing survival. He had grown into a philosopher, one who not only thought deeply but began writing his thoughts down, shaping them into quiet teachings.

Daniel's views had become bold, brutally honest for many of the friends he had made in Sweden. His philosophy often clashed with popular opinion. When people around him believed in what they saw in the media, Daniel challenged them to think otherwise. His views on politics, religion, and global conflicts were often the exact opposite of the average citizen. And when people found no way to counter his arguments, they often threw one line at him like a stone:

"Why are you even here then?"

"Think like us or stay away from us."

Daniel saw this as a fundamental problem today.

People in India and Pakistan often romanticized Europe. They believed Europeans were free, well-educated, critical thinkers. They imagined a land of freedom of speech and intellectual liberty.

But Daniel's lived experience told a different story.

He believed that Europeans, in general, were not as free in their expression as Indians. In India, if the price of milk doubles in six months, people pour into the streets and protest. In Sweden, the same crisis would be met with quiet frustration discussed politely at work during fika, over coffee and cake. No one would march. No one would shout.

Europeans had, over time, become too dependent on their media. Even when the news was obviously false, people believed it without resistance. It was as though progress had made them passive. While countries like India and China were building infrastructure at lightning speed, many European nations had slowed down. Their comfort had turned into complacency.

Daniel observed that students in Europe were more focused on parties than studying. A decline in educational passion and hunger for innovation was visible but ignored. The signs of danger were there, but few could hear the approaching footsteps.

And then, there was the geopolitics.

Europe was geographically connected to Russia, sharing a massive border. Yet, most Europeans were taught to love America an ocean away and hate Russia. To Daniel, it was madness. The belief that Russia must be destroyed or weakened to protect Europe was deeply rooted. But he wondered:

Why not make yourself strong, instead of weakening your neighbor?

If we imagine being born European which, of course, is not something one can choose, we might ask a simple question:

Why are Europeans afraid of Russia? Why do they cling to America as their ally instead of considering a partnership with the neighboring giant?

Ask the average person on the street and you'll rarely receive a logical answer.

Most won't say it aloud, but the truth is clear fear.

They fear Russia because it is a military power. Because it has history. Because it is not a distant nation on another continent, but a towering presence just beyond the border. They fear that without unity, without NATO, Russia could attack.

But why would Russia attack?

What does Europe possess that Russia doesn't already have? Land? No. Resources? Russia has them in abundance. Technology? Influence? Culture? Perhaps. But even then, the fear doesn't come from reason, it comes from history, from propaganda, from the stories people are taught to believe.

And this is what Daniel had begun to understand:

Fear is the oldest weapon.

Fear is the thread sewn into every scenario crafted by those who control the world, the media, politics, the powerful.

It is fear that justifies budgets, borders, weapons, alliances. It is fear that convinces a man to hate another man he has never met. It is fear that keeps people obedient, anxious, easy to mold.

NATO, Daniel believed, was never truly a shield, it was a symbol. A symbol of division dressed as unity. It told the people: *We are safe from them,* without ever explaining *why they* were supposed to be the enemy.

On the other hand, Payja and Pa Shida continued their journey as chemists. They had spent most of their earnings on this obsession. Every time they conducted an experiment; the result was almost the same failure. Just a little more effort, they believed, would bring success. Sometimes they thought they had made gold, but it failed the acid test. Sometimes they missed a single step. Once, Payja didn't tend to the fire properly. Another time, Pa Shida left to milk his cow, and by the time he returned, the fire had gone cold.

Something always went wrong.

Payja ended up selling his land. Pa Shida's farming business collapsed; many of his crops failed, and debts piled up. Now, most of his income has gone toward paying off bank loans. One experiment could cost as much as the price of ten grams of gold. The minerals and chemicals they needed, like arsenic and others, were not only expensive but highly toxic. Buying them wasn't easy. Sometimes, exposure to these chemicals made them sick. Over the years, their lives have grown more and more miserable.

Meanwhile, Daniel had spent nearly ten years in Sweden. He worked hard, earned well, built his own house, bought land, and supported Kala's family regularly. While he grew financially and personally, Payja and Pa Shida lost everything. They were now deep in debt. Payja had no business left; he had turned his living room into a small grocery shop. He sold vegetables and basic items. His son had to leave school because they couldn't afford the fees. If his son went to school, they couldn't afford food.

Daniel could have helped, but he didn't.

To Daniel, help isn't about giving food or money. Help is only meaningful when someone is ready to change. If a person isn't willing to abandon destructive habits, then any help given becomes a curse. Once, Payja called Daniel for money to pay the police. There had been a family quarrel, and someone had filed a complaint. In Pakistan, no matter how small the issue, once it reaches the police, money must be paid to settle it.

Daniel refused to help.

He believed that helping someone in such situations only enables more problems. When people know someone will always rescue them, they misuse that sense of security. They feel free to act without consequence. It's a sickness in societies like India and Pakistan. For example, a son knows that no matter what he does, his father, who works a powerful government job, will save him. First, he commits small wrongs. Then bigger ones. If a father never supports his son in wrongdoing, that son might never walk the path of crime at all.

Life works the same way.

When we stay in hotels, we waste things freely, towels, soaps, toilet paper. We take long showers. We run the air conditioning full blast, leave all the lights on even when we're not in the room. Why? Because we know we've paid for it, and we don't care to save. But at home, we're different. We conserve everything. Not because we care for the environment but because we know we'll pay the bill.

That's how human behavior works.

If we help people every time they make a mess, without asking them to change, we don't lift them, we anchor them deeper. True help begins only when the other person is ready to receive it with awareness and responsibility.

Rani was happy now, settled in her marriage. She used to visit Payja often in the early days, but slowly, Payja began losing interest in her.

One day, she came to see him again. As always, they were upstairs.

"I miss you very much," said Payja.

"Me too," Rani replied softly.

"Where have you left our son?" asked Payja.

"He's with Saleem at the juice shop," she answered.

"Saleem?" Payja snapped. "He's a child molester. Always luring kids with candies. You shouldn't leave our boy with him."

"He won't touch him," she said quickly. "He knows who the real father is."

Tension filled the room. Breath came heavier. Dry lips searched for moisture. There was a strange rhythm in their heartbeats, like silent music. Rani's hair floated in the air like sand carried by the breeze, only to fall back and kiss the shore, losing its dryness.

Waves could be felt inside, soft but urgent. Her body moved slowly at first, as if remembering something it once knew. The doors of desire were wide open, waiting for the one who had long gone. The door itself waited for his return.

But on the other hand, Payja was struggling, his body no longer obeying. Once a shark, now the fish was lifeless. He tried to awaken it, tried to feel something, anything but it was like a dead snake poked by a curious boy with a stick. It did not move.

Even when the door was open, a dead snake could not crawl in. A dead fish could not feast on the fruit of life. A key is only useful when it's made of iron, not wax. A wax key breaks at the lock.

The fight was on. Rani waited. The waves hit the shore, loud and desperate but the shore didn't respond. Not even a trembling.

She tried again to open the lock with the wax key, but it snapped. Broken. Useless.

She had a better fish at home now.

"You don't love me anymore," she said, her voice hollow.

"I do love you," said Payja, "but my body doesn't allow this anymore."

Rani stood. Adjusted her scarf. And left. She never came back.

Chapter 13

AGHORI

Kala was taken into custody and sent to prison. Police asked him for his identity, but he couldn't provide one. Although his accent didn't reveal that he was from Pakistan, and there was no sign to prove he was a terrorist, they still needed evidence that he was truly Indian.

His fingerprints didn't help. He wasn't on any records.

In India, millions live without official identity, so it's not unusual to find someone without an Aadhaar card, but finding such a person in Kashmir was suspicious. In Muslim-majority areas, checks are strict, and authorities rarely spare anyone they suspect, especially minorities.

Inspector Ram, the officer investigating Kala, was known for his cruelty and fake encounters.

"Where were you born?" asked Ram.

"I was born in Punjab," replied Kala.

"Punjab is big. Where in Punjab?"

"Amritsar," said Kala.

He had chosen Amritsar because it was close to the border, and his Punjabi accent matched the local tone. It was believable.

"But your fingerprints aren't in the system. What about your family?" Ram asked.

"I don't know. They left me on the street when I was four. I survived alone," Kala lied smoothly. He was good at making up stories.

"Impossible. You're lying. You're a terrorist. Maybe from Pakistan!" shouted Ram.

"No! I am Indian!" Kala cried.

They tortured him for days. Beat him. Starved him. His fingernails were ripped out. He could barely walk when Inspector Ram came back to his cell one morning.

"I have an offer for you," Ram said, standing with hands behind his back.

"There's a case. A robbery. A shop was looted and burned. We don't know who did it. If you accept the crime, you'll go to prison but when you're released, you'll be someone. You'll have an identity card, documents, fingerprints, and a police record. You'll be able to get an Aadhaar card. A passport. A new life."

Kala listened, confused but desperate.

"Okay," he whispered. "But please, no more beatings. I'm hungry."

From that moment, he was treated kindly. Given food. Clothes. A cigarette.

The next day, Inspector Ram returned with papers. He took Kala's fingerprints and signatures. Everything was written in Hindi; Kala couldn't understand a word.

That afternoon, someone came to see him in the cell. A man handed him cigarettes and said, "When you're released, come to Chaudhary Saab. Ask anyone at this address."

The following morning, Kala was taken to court. Lawyers were whispering, papers being shuffled. The judge entered, a heavy-set man with black glasses, looking down at Kala over his file.

The courtroom settled.

"My lord," said the prosecution, "Mr. Kala Agnihotri is a dangerous criminal. Three months ago, he murdered a local political leader. He fled to Srinagar and stayed in a hotel; we have proof. This knife, recovered from him, was the murder weapon. He confessed. We request punishment under IPC 302 and 307 at least life imprisonment."

Even the defense lawyer nodded.

The judge turned to Kala.

"Have you given this confession?"

Kala stared blankly.

He thought it was robbery. That's what Inspector Ram said.

But murder?

Still, he couldn't change his story now. He had no choice.

"Did you kill Mr. Prasad?" asked the judge.

"Yes," Kala said quietly. "I didn't like him. I was drunk. I hit him for fun. He died."

"Hit for fun?" the judge raised an eyebrow.

"I thought it was a stick. It was a knife."

The defense quickly added, "My lord, I believe his mental condition is not stable."

No one objected.

The judge paused, then spoke:

"Very well. I sentence the accused to ten years imprisonment under IPC 302. During his sentence, he shall undergo mental health evaluations and receive treatment at state expense.

Everyone nodded. The courtroom cleared.

As Kala was led out, Inspector Ram clapped him lightly on the back.

"You did well. Thank you for not changing your mind. When your time is up, come to me. My station's doors are open for you."

And just like that, Kala became a ghost, vanished from his past, swallowed by a new false name, buried in a prison record that didn't belong to him.

Kala was sent to prison. He had to serve ten years.

When he entered, it wasn't a shock. Pakistani and Indian prisons looked nearly the same. The only difference he noticed, Indian prisons were dirtier. It wasn't just a thought, but something he observed with his own eyes. Years ago, he had spent a week in a Pakistani prison after a conflict with Payja and some others. That memory helped him walk into this one with a strange familiarity.

In this prison too, he was shown a kind of respect. By the next day, word had spread that Kala had killed a well-known politician. In prisons, new arrivals are often judged by their crimes. Although by law inmates are not supposed to know each other's cases, that law is never respected. Everyone knows why everyone is there.

A dark truth about prison life: many inmates are used as sex slaves. It's not spoken about openly, but it's considered part of the "comforts" or power dynamics inside. If a young and good-looking prisoner doesn't want to fight back or get into daily conflict, he often chooses to be under the protection of a stronger prisoner by offering himself sexually in return for safety. It's a common survival tactic. If one refuses this path and still doesn't want to fight, the torment never stops. Complaining means getting transferred, but nothing truly changes. Eventually, every inmate has to choose to fight or submit.

Some fight and earn peace. Some surrender and become someone's "bitch".

Kala was spared. Not by luck but by appearance. His face, his roughness, and his lack of charm protected him. No one was interested in using him. He was safe, unwanted, and in that respect.

One evening, a man approached him.

Nearly naked, long-haired, wild-eyed, he looked like someone from another world. The man stood in front of Kala and greeted him softly, "Namaste. I know who you are."

Kala frowned. "What do you mean? Who am I?"

"You're a traveler," the man said. "You're here for a purpose. I can feel it in your energy. You've come from the West. You've witnessed violence. A lot of it. You've done wrong. And now… now you seek something precious."

"Stop!" Kala barked, startled.

But the man didn't flinch. "Don't be afraid," he said gently. "No one can harm you. You've been chosen. You're here for something greater, something you don't yet understand."

Something shifted in Kala. He listened.

"I'm sad," Kala admitted. "Everything is broken."

"All your sadness, your suffering, your searching, it ends here," said the man. "You have come to the right place. Your true journey begins now… and it will never end."

The man turned to leave, his voice trailing behind him. "Your family, your child, every bond has already found peace. You will see. You will understand. Soon."

And then, he vanished into the shadows of his cell.

"I'll come to you again," he said softly. "In the morning."

Kala looked around and found a corner for himself in the overcrowded prison cell. It wasn't easy to sleep, there were too many bodies, too little space but Kala managed. He wasn't just a prisoner. He was the man who had "killed a famous politician," and that label brought a strange kind of respect.

The next day, one of his cellmates, a wiry man named Deva, leaned in and asked, "What was the Aghori talking to you about?"

Kala turned his head, confused. "Who? Aghori? Who is that?"

Deva smirked. "You don't know? I figured. That half-naked man who came to you last night that's the Aghori."

Kala furrowed his brow. "Aghori? That's his name?"

"No," Deva chuckled. "It's not a name, it's what he is. An Aghori is someone who follows Lord Shiva, Mahadev. They live outside society. They reject rules. They walk where others fear to look."

Kala still looked puzzled. "But why doesn't he wear clothes? Why is he always dirty, with ash all over his body?"

Deva laughed. "Where have you been living all your life, brother?

"Even filth. Even corpses. Even madness. They're not trying to look holy; they're looking *through* the illusion. Most of us live our whole lives afraid of death, afraid of what others think. Aghoris… they don't care. They want truth, not comfort."

Kala looked towards the far wall where the ash-covered man had vanished into his cell. His mind was quiet. For a moment, his crime, his fear, his future, all felt like someone else's story.

"Why was he talking to me?" he asked.

Deva smiled.

"Because he saw something in you. Maybe he knows your journey isn't over. Maybe... it's just begun."

One thing I can tell you for sure," Deva said, his tone lower now, almost reverent, "that Aghori is not a normal man. He's like a saint, he knows things. He sees what we can't. Feels what we're not even capable of sensing. He can see the past, the future... beyond what's visible."

Kala listened in awe. Ten years in this cell, ten years with strange men and darker nights, and perhaps he thought, ten years to learn.

That night, as the cell sank into silence, Kala couldn't sleep. His first real night inside. The smell of sweat, of damp clothes and rusted metal filled the air. And then came the sounds strange, soft at first: *Se... ah... ha... ah...* A whimper. A whisper. Bodies moving too close, breath quickening. The floor beneath him trembled faintly, like a heartbeat under stone.

He understood. This would be routine here. Desire finds its way even in chains, even in darkness. No privacy, no shame, no boundaries. Just nights, long and hollow.

Morning came. They all rose and rushed to queue for breakfast. A mess of metal trays, long lines, loud shouts. No tables, just the floor, wherever you could find a patch to sit and eat.

Kala sat cross-legged, swallowing dry rice and lentils when the Aghori appeared.

He crouched beside him, eyes glowing in the early light. "Mahadev sent you here," he said without a greeting. "Ask me what was in your heart last night. Ask me anything. Only for you, your doubts will be cleared. Not for others. Only you."

Kala paused, rice still in his fingers. "Tell me about my family," he asked.

"They are well," the Aghori replied calmly. "I see your daughter. She's eating mango and rice. Soon she'll start school. There is food in your house. Your wife is smiling. She is not sad."

They think you are dead.

Kala's eyes widened. "How do you know this? Why… why do they think I'm dead?"

"You know why," the Aghori said, and stood up to leave. "You already know how and why."

And just like that, he was gone.

Kala sat frozen. The truth struck him like a stone in the chest, he had fled during the mission, and the others had died. The organization, of course, must have assumed he had died with them.

Maybe that was for the best.

His family wouldn't have to wait ten long years. They would mourn, then heal. Move on. Live.

And his friends Payja, Daniel, they would keep their promise. They would take care of his family.

Kala believed every word the Aghori had spoken.

"How could he know these things?" he whispered to himself. "How?"

And a thought sparked in his mind, clear and burning *I will learn. I will become like him. I will learn to see. And one day, I'll know the truth about the water of the 22 Kunds too.*

Kala had started following the Aghori like a shadow. In the dusty, suffocating routine of prison, the Aghori had become a light, unpredictable, wild, but glowing with a strange truth. They talked for hours in the corners no one sat under windows where the sunlight broke in silently, like secrets.

The Aghori wasn't in prison for theft, murder, or violence. He was in for truth.

He had no official identity—no Aadhaar, no ration card, nothing that tied him to the world outside the ash on his skin and the gods in his breath. And when a curious inspector once demanded answers, the Aghori gave them warnings.

It happened in the police station before he was locked up. The inspector, loud and arrogant, mocked him.

"If you're really a saint," the inspector said, "tell me about my family. My wife. My children. Tell us the truth. Prove you know something."

The Aghori folded his hands and bowed his head. "Please," he said, "ask me in private. The truth… might hurt."

But the inspector laughed. "Tell me here, now, in front of everyone."

The Aghori sighed. Then he spoke.

"You have no child. You never had one. You cannot. The children in your house belong to another man. Your wife is happy. She has everything she needs, money… and two men. One who pays for the house. One who warms her bed."

A hush fell over the room. The laughter died.

The inspector's face turned a dark, violent red. Rage flooded his body like boiling water. He grabbed the Aghori by the neck and beat him mercilessly day after day. No court. No lawyers. Just fists and silence.

Then he filled a false case against him. Murder. Fraud. Insanity. Whatever he could think of.

And the Aghori was sent here.

Now, he walked barefoot through the prison yard, speaking to ants, watching clouds, whispering verses to the wind. He never complained. Never ask why. When Kala asked him how he survived all of this, the Aghori smiled.

"The world punishes truth-tellers, Kala," he said, "but only for a while. After that, it listens."

Kala had surrendered himself to the Divine.

Not to a religion, not to a name, but to something higher. To the pulse behind the stars, to the breath between the trees, to that quiet presence that watches without judgement. Yes, he was born into a Muslim family, but to him, God was not confined to one name, one face, one ritual. Whether called Allah, Jesus, Ram, Mahadev, or Jehovah, Kala bowed with the same reverence.

His heart was simple. And that simplicity made space.

When a heart is unburdened by prejudice, ready to receive without question, the Divine rushes in like water into a hollowed cup. The Divine, after all, is always giving. But only the open can receive.

Blessings are not scarce; readiness is.

The Aghori had once told him: *"To know the light, you must sit with your own darkness. To receive the gift, you must become empty."*

And Kala understood now.

He had begun to meditate, silently, in the same cross-legged posture he saw the Aghori take at dawn. At first, it was difficult, his thoughts scattered like dry leaves in the wind. But slowly, with each breath, silence came. Then stillness. Then… something else.

Peace.

In the chaos of the prison, amid the stench and screams, Kala had become another Aghori. Not in appearance, but in spirit.

He no longer asked when he would leave, when justice would arrive, or if his name would ever be cleared.

He had found his truth in surrender. He had found his freedom behind bars.

Chapter 14

BLIND JOURNEY

Daniel finally agreed to travel to India to accomplish two things. First, find the herbs, minerals, and the water of the 22 kunds. Second, perhaps even more important to him, to find the grave of his martyred friend, Kala.

He had heard that Mujahideen who are killed by the Indian Army are buried somewhere, and most of the time their names are carved on the gravestones. That thought stayed with him.

But the problem was clear. For a Pakistani-born person, getting an Indian visa was a huge task. The only plus Daniel had been that he was not a Muslim but a Christian and for Christians, it's always a bit easier to get an Indian visa, even if you were born in Pakistan.

Daniel, however, had more than one thing in his heart. He also wanted to visit the great Hindu temples spread across the country. So, when he applied for an Indian visa at the Stockholm embassy, he chose his purpose of visit as "temple pilgrimage." It was a perfect excuse. Temples are everywhere in India from the snowy north to the tropical south. That excuse would allow him to travel freely and widely. And he genuinely wanted to learn more about Hinduism too.

Daniel was the kind of man who always tried to squeeze the last drop of juice from the lemon. His vision now was crystal clear: visit all over India, search for Kala's grave, collect rare herbs, chemicals, and the sacred water of 22 kunds, and study the diversity of India's cultures, differences shaped by religion, language, and ethnicity.

His new friends in Stockholm thought it was a bad idea to visit India. Most Pakistanis carry a quiet fear, something might go wrong in India, and they could end up paying for it. If you're from Pakistan and happen to be in the wrong place at the wrong time like a city where a terrorist act or a bomb blast occurs, you'll likely be the first to be arrested. It doesn't matter if you're innocent. It doesn't matter why you came. It could take years before anyone even believes you're not guilty.

It had happened before. A few Pakistanis who visited India from abroad were arrested under suspicion of spying and some of them were still lost in the system.

But Daniel knew one thing for sure: *he was clean.* A true believer in God. A man with purpose.

He knew exactly why he was going. And despite what everyone around him thought, he felt no fear.

In fact, there was something even more surprising about him, something no one in his village back home would understand. Daniel deeply admired Narendra Modi, the Indian Prime Minister. While most Pakistanis hated Modi and accused him of spreading religious hatred, Daniel saw something else. He saw simplicity. He saw a man who had risen from nothing. A saint in politics, perhaps.

Of course, he couldn't deny the truth either, yes, India was heading down a dangerous path. Once known proudly as a secular state, India now appeared to be moving in the direction Pakistan had already gone into the darkness of religious extremism. That was the only flaw Daniel could see in Modi's

India. But otherwise? India was growing. Flourishing. Becoming stronger every day.

When Daniel wrote a letter to the Embassy with application for the visa. He addressed the ambassador directly.

He explained that he wasn't an ordinary traveler. He was a researcher, a spiritual seeker, someone who admired Indian culture and had a deep love for India. He even wrote that he believed the partition of *Bharat* in 1947 was a great mistake, and that, in truth, he felt more Indian than Pakistani. After all, his father was born in India.

He ended his letter with three bold words:

"Jai Hind."

The letter worked. The message was received.

Daniel was granted a tourist visa to India.

Daniel informed the embassy about his intention to visit Kashmir, as two great Hindu temples stood there: the Vaishno Devi Temple and the Shankaracharya Temple. Surprisingly, he received permission to visit Kashmir legally. He had never heard of any Pakistani visiting Kashmir through legal means before. That alone made him feel like he had achieved something great.

His journey was planned: a flight to Delhi, then a connection from Delhi to Srinagar. From Sweden, the journey to Delhi took around 9 to 10 hours, there were no direct flights. When the plane finally landed in Delhi, the first thing that hit Daniel wasn't the heat or the crowd but the air.

The smell of smog almost knocked him unconscious. The air quality index in Delhi that day was over 350, while in Stockholm it had been just 21. The difference was unimaginable. Breathing suddenly became a task, as if someone had placed a cloth soaked in smoke over his mouth. After ten years of living in clean Nordic air, this was unbearable.

Delhi itself was something else. A place so overwhelming that Daniel felt he couldn't spend even a few hours there. But he had to, his connecting flight to Srinagar was scheduled for the next day.

Finding a hotel has become another challenge. One piece of advice for travelers he learned quickly: **never book cheap hotels in Delhi online.** Unless you're booking a five-star hotel, what they show online and what you find are two different worlds.

The next day, his flight to Srinagar was packed. The plane soared over the mountains, and Daniel felt like he was flying toward a dream. Visiting Kashmir, legally, as a Pakistani-born man, it wasn't just a trip, it was a moment of pride. An achievement. Proof of identity and worth.

When the plane landed in Srinagar, Daniel looked out eagerly.

The first glimpse of Kashmir didn't quite match the image he had painted in his mind. Yes, there were mountains around the airport. Yes, it was scenic. But it wasn't *Jannat*, not the paradise that was so often romanticized in Pakistan.

There are many beautiful places on Earth, Daniel thought. Kashmir is one of them. But it's not *the* one. It's not heaven.

When we carry too many expectations in our mind about something or someone, we often end up disappointed. It's simply human nature. The more we expect, the less satisfied we tend to be. And the less we expect the more joy we find in what comes.

This truth fits into every corner of life.

Take, for example, a football match. We expect our team to win easily because the opponent is weak. But that day, our team loses, and our disappointment feels heavier than it should. On another day, when we expect nothing, our team will surely lose, they end up defeating a stronger opponent. That unexpected victory fills us with immense happiness.

This same pattern repeats in friendships, love, career, politics, even spirituality.

Expectations are like invisible weights we carry them with hope, but they can crush our peace when things don't go the way we imagined.

Daniel stepped into a taxi outside Srinagar airport. The driver, a young man with a trimmed beard, greeted him warmly. As they drove toward the city, Daniel noticed his phone wasn't working.

"You'll need a new SIM," said the driver. "In Kashmir, only postpaid Indian connections work."

"I'll get one then," Daniel replied.

They stopped at a small shop, and the driver helped him purchase a SIM card. During the process, the driver learned that Daniel was originally from Pakistan. The revelation lit up the faces of everyone in the shop, they had never met a Pakistani visitor before.

"That's amazing," Daniel thought.

"I want to ask you something," Daniel said quietly, "but only if you promise to keep my secrets and not put me in trouble."

"Until you're with me, you're safe," the driver replied firmly. "I love Pakistan. You're our guest."

"I'm looking for herb," Daniel said. "It glows in the night. It's called *Jeevani Booti* or *Sanjivani Booti*."

"Okay, my name is Bilal. Save my number first. I'll take you to a good place, and in the evening, we can go look for this herb in the mountains," Bilal offered. "But one thing, you'll have to pay for my time. Driving is how I earn my living."

"Don't worry," Daniel said. "I'll pay."

"Have you booked a hotel?" asked Bilal.

"No." Replied Daniel.

They found a cozy hotel nestled in a quiet part of Srinagar. The landscape was stunning, and the food was excellent. That evening, Bilal drove him out to the mountains. The night was deep and dark, but they found nothing. No herbs glow said Bilal.

"I need one more favor," Daniel said, glancing at his phone.

"What kind?" asked Bilal.

"I want to visit the place where they bury the Shaheed Mujahideen."

"I'll take you," said Bilal. "But why do you want to go there? They only bury Kashmiri Mujahideen in those places."

"I thought maybe Pakistani Mujahideen were buried there too."

"No, my friend," Bilal said, his voice softening. "Pakistanis were always treated as outsiders here. The military never let us bury them on our own. Honestly, most Kashmiris wouldn't accept it either."

"Then where do they bury them?" Daniel asked, a shadow passing over his face.

"I don't know. Maybe they burn the bodies… or throw them into the woods. But not with us."

Daniel was quiet the whole next day. That night, they went asking around, elderly men, herbalists, anyone who might know of the glowing herb, but no one had heard of it. Then something sparked Daniel's mind.

"What if we ask a saint?" he said aloud.

"A saint?" Bilal looked puzzled. "Hindu or Muslim?"

"Hindu," Daniel replied after a moment, recalling the story of the saint from his earlier quest.

"Then we'll go to the temple."

They climbed the hill to the Shankaracharya Temple and waited, hoping to find someone who might know. But Daniel kept thinking, *what does a saint even look like in today's world?*

Just then, he saw a man with a long white beard climbing the hill alone. Daniel greeted him with respectful *Namaste* and explained what he was searching for.

"Incredible," the man said. "You're the second person in my life to speak of this herb. No one in Kashmir talks about it."

He paused, remembering.

"About ten years ago, I met a beggar, hungry, sitting on the roadside. I scolded him, but he said he was starving. I bought him food and offered him work on my farm. He was a good man. I've forgotten his name… but he lived with us for a while. At night, he would climb the hills. One morning, he returned with herbs, glowing herbs. That's how I know they exist."

Daniel listened intently, his heart racing. "Can you take me to your farm? Can you show me where he found them?"

The old man nodded.

He took them to his farm, vast, remote, nestled in the arms of the mountains. And Daniel felt it.

"Can you tell me exactly when and how you saw him returning with those herbs?" asked Daniel curiously.

"I remember clearly. He was coming from that direction," said the old man, pointing his finger toward a distant part of the mountain. "He had something glowing in his hands. It caught my attention because the dogs suddenly started barking, so I stepped out to see what was going on, and that's when I saw him."

The old man paused and then continued thoughtfully, "He never told me why he needed those herbs. Why do you want them?"

Daniel quickly created a story, "I want to use them to make medicine—an ancient remedy for curing cancer."

Daniel didn't really care about gold or money. He had earned enough during his time in Sweden. His true purpose here was deeper: to fulfill his promise, to find his friend's grave, to explore, and perhaps discover much more.

The old man nodded kindly, "Alright, you're welcome to stay here, and if you need anything, feel free to ask."

"Thank you," Daniel said gratefully. "Bilal and I will head in that direction as soon as night falls."

As the old man walked away to tend his cattle, Daniel carefully observed the surrounding mountains. The highest peaks weren't close; reaching them would require considerable effort.

"Maybe we should start walking now," Daniel suggested.

"Alright, let's go," Bilal agreed.

Soon they were ascending the rugged slopes. Bilal advised Daniel to climb sideways. "It makes climbing easier," he explained, "but remember, climbing up is always easier than climbing down."

Daniel couldn't grasp how descending a mountain could be harder than ascending it.

As they continued, Bilal spoke reflectively, "You know, these mountains have witnessed so much violence. The two countries have fought fiercely over Kashmir. In the past, we Kashmiris wanted to join Pakistan, but now we prefer India."

Daniel was shocked. He had spent his entire life believing that Kashmiris desperately wished to become part of Pakistan, yet here was a young Kashmiri expressing the exact opposite.

Bilal continued, "We still love Pakistan as fellow Muslims, but Pakistan has ruined its own country. Their economy has collapsed, their global reputation is damaged, and we've started to hate their military establishment."

"Aha," Daniel remarked thoughtfully. "So, you also understand the core of our problems. I thought only we Pakistanis knew exactly what's wrong with our country. I'm surprised a young man from Kashmir knows this too."

Bilal responded sincerely, "We love Pakistan mainly because it's an Islamic country, whereas India isn't."

"Oh my God," Daniel said, almost amused. "How do you even know there is true Islam in Pakistan?"

Daniel continued speaking, "You know, Bilal, tell me a few things, do you drink alcohol? How many people in Srinagar drink alcohol?"

"No, I don't drink," replied Bilal firmly. "If we find a Muslim drinking alcohol in Srinagar, we beat him."

"Alright," Daniel continued, "Is it possible to find a prostitute in Srinagar? I mean, a local prostitute?"

"No, absolutely not," said Bilal quickly. "In Srinagar, you can't even bring a local girl to a hotel. No hotel will allow a local girl without family."

"Now let me tell you about Pakistan," Daniel began. "In Pakistan, I honestly don't know a single friend who doesn't drink alcohol. Almost all my friend's drink. I also know many people who regularly use drugs, especially hashish. You can easily buy hashish in any city. In every big city, in nearly every street, you can find prostitutes. They're everywhere, and you can take any girl to any hotel, no one will question you. Even people with long beards commit all these sins, they pray five times a day. Do you think this is what an Islamic country looks like?" Daniel asked.

"No, it definitely isn't," Bilal replied, astonished. "Are you telling me the truth?"

"Why would I lie to you?" Daniel said openly. "I've seen and done these things all my life when I lived in Pakistan."

By now they had reached higher up the mountain. A cool and gentle breeze blew, softly moving Daniel's hair as if a lover touched him tenderly. Darkness had fully settled around them. Daniel looked around carefully and suggested, "Let's sit here for a while and observe."

They sat down. Daniel closed his eyes and started praying silently, as he often did at new places. He wanted the mountains to bear witness to his prayers. It was both fun and meaningful, a kind of tradition. He had read in books that many great saints meditated and prayed on mountains. Mahadev meditated on high altitudes; Moses climbed Mount Sinai; Jesus went into the hills near Jericho; even Muhammad sought solitude in the mountains. Daniel wondered, what was so special about mountains? Perhaps because fewer people reached these heights? Maybe mountains were free from human negativity? Maybe God preferred to stay away from crowded human spaces?

Then it struck his silence.

"Yes," Daniel thought, "Silence is God's language." Silence was how God spoke. God didn't need a tongue or a physical form. God was beyond all physical limitations, limitless, vast, and silent.

A sudden, strange electric sensation surged through Daniel's body. His eyes snapped open, and he saw a faint glow in the distance. It was steady, not flickering like fireflies, but softly glowing. "Let's go," he said quickly.

Bilal immediately followed. They moved swiftly toward the mysterious glow. After a long walk, they finally reached the herb. Daniel quickly collected as much as he could, stuffing it into his bag.

On their way back down, Bilal smiled knowingly, "Now, tell me, Daniel, is it going down easier or harder?"

Daniel felt it clearly now descending was indeed harder. Going down required controlling movements, carefully stopping momentum at each step. By the time they returned to the farm, Daniel fully understood what Bilal had meant.

Daniel's next destination was to find the sacred water. He had carefully packed the glowing herbs and sent them by post to Payja. After dispatching the parcel, he called Payja, who was extremely delighted with the progress. The only things they now required were sacred water and certain rare poisons. Obtaining pure poisons in India wouldn't be too challenging, but finding the sacred water was another matter.

Daniel traveled to the famous Vishnu Devi Temple, hoping to meet someone knowledgeable there. At the temple, he noticed a group of Rishis and some devotees of Mahadev engaged in quiet discussions. Daniel approached one of them respectfully and asked, "Do you know anything about the water of twenty-two kunds? Does anyone here know about it?"

The Rishi paused thoughtfully for a moment and then called out to his companion, "Kumarey, come here! Aren't those twenty-two wells located in Rameshwaram?"

Kumarey responded promptly, "Yes, precisely! I visited Rameshwaram last year. The twenty-two kunds you're speaking about are definitely there."

Turning back to Daniel, the Rishi explained, "The twenty-two kunds are sacred wells in Rameshwaram, each containing water with unique properties. It's believed that bathing or using water from all these wells purifies the soul, washes away sins, and brings divine blessings. Every well has a distinct spiritual significance and is said to possess unique mineral properties, offering profound spiritual and physical purification."

Daniel listened carefully, realizing he had found another crucial piece of his puzzle. He was now determined, Rameshwaram would be his next destination.

Chapter 15

NEW DESTINATION

Kala had finally found the answers he'd been searching for; his life had changed dramatically. The influence of the Aghori had profoundly altered his perspective during his years in prison. Day after day, he meditated diligently, transforming himself into someone he never imagined he could become.

Due to his exemplary behavior, Kala was released earlier than his original sentence. He had performed labor during his imprisonment and was astonished when he received wages for his work, money he hadn't even known existed. As he left the prison, he asked an official how he could obtain an Aadhaar card. The prison had issued him documents stating his imprisonment and confirming his release after seven years. With these papers, he walked straight to the Aadhaar office. There, they took his fingerprints and photograph, and soon he was issued an Aadhaar card, officially becoming an Indian citizen.

The weather was mild as Kala set out, wandering aimlessly in an unknown direction. Among the few belongings returned to him was the glowing herb he had collected years ago, yet now it meant nothing to him. His journey, his prison years, and the teachings of the Aghori had brought him to a different understanding. He was no longer the same man who had desperately sought gold and riches. Instead, he had found inner peace, something far more precious.

As he walked along the road, he noticed a poor woman begging near a hospital, clutching a small child in her arms. Without hesitation, Kala handed her all the money he'd received from his labor in prison, leaving himself completely penniless. Poverty didn't frighten him anymore; in prison, he had learned how to meditate calmly in a yogic posture for hours, to live without food for days, and to tune into subtle sounds and vibrations that most others never heard.

Kala began walking steadily southward. He moved like a straight line, unwavering and determined, undeterred by any obstacle. He felt guided by something invisible, drawn toward an unknown destination. It was as though some powerful force or spiritual current was pulling him along, much like the way a moth is irresistibly attracted to a candle's flame though the flame may burn it, still, the moth cannot resist its call.

Two days had passed, yet Kala did not pause anywhere. After walking continuously, he came across a village. As he passed through, a grand house caught his attention, compelling his feet to halt at its doorway. Kala stood still; his gaze fixed on the entrance.

Soon, a beautiful woman stepped out of the house and looked towards him. She observed the man standing before her, his body covered with ashes, long unshaven hair and beard, almost naked, a true Aghori in appearance. She respectfully opened the door wider and said, "Please, Guru ji, come inside."

Within minutes, Kala was comfortably seated at a table, provided with food and water. The entire household had gathered around him, intrigued by this unexpected visitor.

After Kala finished his meal, he asked gently, "You've provided me with food and kindness, please, ask anything in return."

The woman, clearly the head of the family, spoke up with hesitation, "Guru ji, if you don't mind, could you grant me something I desperately want?"

Kala replied calmly, "I have nothing to give, but Mahadev can grant anything."

Tears filled the woman's eyes as she quietly implored, "Please, come inside with me."

Kala rose and silently followed her into the inner room. There, on a bed, lay her young husband, struggling through what seemed like his last breaths.

"We have plenty of money, wealth, everything one could wish for in this world," she sobbed, "but all our wealth couldn't save his life. The doctors have given up hope. They say he won't survive."

Kala gazed thoughtfully at the man and then spoke with calm certainty, "He will not die."

Everyone stared at Kala, their eyes filled with doubt. The woman replied anxiously, "Guru ji, perhaps today is his last day."

Without hesitation, Kala took a small number of dried herbs from his bag. It crumbled to dust in his palm. He requested honey, mixed the powder carefully into it, and gently placed the mixture into the dying man's mouth.

Turning towards the woman, Kala said quietly, "Now I must go. He will live. His time has not yet come, he has a long life ahead."

The woman, astonished and hopeful, pleaded, "Then please stay with us a few days. Witness yourself how he recovers."

Kala looked deeply into her eyes, "Are you doubting?"

"No, Guru ji," the woman quickly answered, lowering her gaze respectfully.

"Then have no fear. He will live," Kala assured her, stepping out through the doorway.

Despite her persistent attempts to make him stay, Kala could not linger. He began walking again, continuing his endless journey.

Kala continued walking till nightfall, eventually stopping at the summit of a high hill. There he built a fire and seated himself in a yoga position. The entire night passed as he remained seated still, serene, eyes closed in meditation. He could rest deeply without lying down; perhaps sleep was no longer necessary for him.

Early in the morning, as sunlight gently touched the hill, Kala sensed a presence around him. A crowd of people had quietly gathered, sitting nearby, waiting patiently for him to open his eyes so they might speak. When Kala finally opened his eyes, he immediately recognized the woman he had met the previous day and beside her sat the man who had seemed on the verge of death. Now the man appeared strong and healthy. Kala smiled gently.

The woman spoke loudly, joyfully, "Jai ho, Guru ji! After you left yesterday something miraculous happened. My husband suddenly found strength returning to his body. Within moments, he stood up, walking as if he had never been sick. By evening, he was completely healed, filled with energy. We spent the entire night celebrating your blessing. Early this morning, we began searching in the direction you traveled. Now we have found you, just as we hoped. My husband's sickness is completely gone. We came here only to thank you and invite you once again to stay a few days in our village."

Kala gently shook his head, responding softly, "My path isn't meant for villages or crowds anymore. I have a journey, a direction I must follow. Why should I stay when you no longer have any troubles? Go back home and enjoy your life."

The woman, moved deeply, had tears in her eyes. Quietly, she reached into her bag, took out a small cloth purse, and placed it reverently at Kala's feet. "Guru ji," she said, her voice emotionally, "this is my bhiksha, an offering for you. Please accept it."

Kala looked down at the purse thoughtfully. "What would I do with this? I walk barefoot, carrying nothing. How would I keep this with me on my endless journey?"

"Please keep it, Guru ji," the woman insisted gently. "Perhaps one day it will be useful."

Kala finally picked up the purse. Overwhelmed with gratitude, the woman and her husband lovingly touched Kala's feet, repeating, "Jai ho, Guru ji," before turning away and heading home.

Kala felt the weight of the purse. Curiosity stirred him to open it, revealing inside nearly a kilo of gold. He smiled, his gaze lifting toward the sky, as he quietly spoke, "Why now, Mahadev? Now, this gold is nothing but a stone to me. When I yearned for it and needed it desperately, it never came. Now that I have no desire or use for it, you have placed it in my hands. Why?"

Kala began walking again. He passed through many villages and cities until he reached a larger town, where he found a place for abandoned elderly people. It was an ashram. Quietly, Kala dropped the entire kilo of gold into the ashram's donation box and walked away. He couldn't carry that weight any longer; it was nothing more than a burden to him now.

Someone saw him doing this. When the people at the ashram discovered the gold, they were shocked. They hurried to chase after Kala and found him sitting under a tree just outside the city, in the scorching heat.

"Guru ji, we came to request you to come with us. Please stay at our ashram," they said.

"Why should I stay with you?" Kala replied calmly. "I don't need a roof or a room. I can sleep under this tree tonight."

"No, Guru ji," the man pleaded, "you have helped us so much. At least give us a chance to show our love to you. Let us cook something for you."

"Alright," said Kala, "if you want to feed me, I will eat."

He followed them back. They gave him warm food and fresh milk. Kala ate, thanked the Divine, and asked, "Is there anything I can do for you in return?"

"You have already done more than enough," an old man replied. "The gold you donated will keep us running for years."

"Are you sure you don't need anything?" Kala asked again.

One of the old men, hesitating at first, finally said, "Guru ji, our Pandit Ramdev is very sick. Would you mind taking a look at him?"

They led Kala to the pandit, who was pale and weak. Kala took out a small amount of the herb from his pouch, mashed it in his hand, and asked for some honey. Mixing the herb with honey, he placed it gently in the pandit's mouth.

"He'll be fine," said Kala.

"Thank you, Guru ji," the old man said. "We also have a woman here who's been suffering from something unknown."

Kala looked at her calmly and said, "She is fine," and turned to leave.

They all begged him to stay but Kala couldn't. He never could. Almost a year passed, and he finally reached the southern part of India, close to the sea. He could feel the difference between the north and the south.

Eventually, he arrived at a grand temple. He saw thousands of devotees coming and going. Inside, surrounded by chanting and incense, Kala found answers to the questions that had haunted him for years.

He hadn't known he could heal anyone. He never believed he could. But now he understood, *it wasn't his power that healed, it was their faith.* The energy didn't come from him. It came from the divine. It flowed through love and devotion, not through any religion.

God is love, he realized. And no matter what name one gives, Jesus, Allah, Mahadev, Jehovah, it all leads back to love. Whoever holds love in their heart will ultimately find the divine.

He also discovered something more profound: he could see through people's souls. He could see the divine and the devil within them. There was no third path. Only two forces controlled a human being, either divine or demonic. There was no true middle way.

Right and wrong? Merely perspectives.

If a man chooses the wrong, the dark path, or even the devil himself, it does not offend God. The divine does not fear darkness. What matters are the *consequences.* Every action has one.

Choosing the devil's way leads to destruction. Choosing the divine path brings peace, productivity, and love.

That is the truth of life: we are free. Free to walk the road of life or death, love or hate. There's no "wrong" in choosing but we must be ready to face what comes.

Plant wheat, reap wheat. Plant wild grass, reap wild grass.

The outcome never changes, repeat the experiment a million times, it remains the same. It is not punishment. It is law. It is nature.

Both wheat and wild grass are part of balance. Both tigers and deer must live. Both snakes and frogs are needed. Both good and evil create the beauty of life.

Kala was now a well-known Aghori in a city with a large temple. He had no clothes on his body, no home, no belongings, only a small cloth bag holding the same herb he had brought years ago from the mountains. And one more thing: ashes.

The story of those ashes was sacred.

A year ago, when he was still in prison, he had spent years with his Aghori friend, his mentor, and his brother in silence. One day, everything shifted.

"I think I will be leaving soon," the Aghori said quietly, gazing into the void.

"Leaving where?" Kala asked. "How will you leave your body? Isn't that in the hands of the Creator?"

"Yes," said the Aghori, smiling. "But you will understand what that means when you become one with the Creator yourself."

He continued, "Listen carefully. On Poornima, the full moon night, I will leave. I've already told the jailor that you will perform my cremation. You will light the pyre, sit there, and wait until my body becomes ash. Gather what remains. If you find any bones, offer them to Ma Ganga. The rest of the ashes rub them on your body. Don't wash them off for seven days. And keep some in a jar. You'll know when you need them. I won't tell you, but the ashes will."

At that time, the Aghori was smiling, peaceful, and strong.

"What am I going to do with your ashes?" Kala had asked.

"I told you, "Said the Aghori. "You'll know. The ashes will speak."

On the night of the full moon, the Aghori sat in a deep yogic posture and began his final meditation. He looked calm, still, like a statue of Lord Shiva himself.

The next morning, he didn't show up for food. Kala already knew.

He found him still in his meditation pose but lifeless.

The jailors allowed Kala to carry out the last rites. He stayed by the burning pier all day. When the flames were cold, he gathered the ashes as instructed. He rubbed them onto his body.

And then something happened.

Suddenly, he saw the same face on every person around him. A face bathed in blue the face of Mahadev. He couldn't distinguish one person from another except by their voice. The cook, the guard, the sweepers, the criminals, everyone looked like Mahadev.

"Why?" Kala whispered to the sky. "How can I let you cook for me? How can I let you sweep floors or stare at me from every direction?"

Even his own reflection had changed. He was no longer Kala.

He was Mahadev.

He had to learn to treat himself with the same reverence he offered to others. He saw himself in others, and others in himself. He began to treat everyone as if they were divine. For seven days, he wore those ashes. During those seven days, his life transformed from that of an ordinary man to something far beyond.

People he touched were healed. He never announced it but he observed.

Still, he knew he couldn't defy nature. People will fall ill. Some will heal; some will die. Everyone must leave their body one day. The soul must find its next journey. He could not stop death. Nor did he want to.

Suffering was a necessary part of the journey. It made life meaningful. Without pain, struggle, or loss life would become dull, flat, without color. A life without challenges would be like a song with no rhythm.

He understood the deeper truths of life.

After seven days, he washed himself. The visions faded. People looked normal again. The illusion dissolved but the wisdom remained.

A few days later, the jailor came to him.

"I have good news," he said, beaming. "You're going home. You were sentenced to ten years, but because of your good conduct, you're being released after seven."

"Where will I go?" Kala asked softly. "What is outside? Where is outside?"

The jailor laughed. "The world is big, my friend. You can go anywhere."

The next day, Kala was handed his few belongings and released.

Now, he lives under a tree near the city temple. People came every day to touch his feet. He never asked for anything. At night, he sat in deep yogic posture, barely sleeping. Each morning, he bathed inside the temple and returned to his tree. Someone always came to offer him food. He accepted it quietly and ate with gratitude.

His life was as simple as the breeze that passed through the branches of the tree above him.

Chapter 16

THE CONCLUSION

In all these years, while Payja and Pa Shida were busy with their experiments but never succeeded, Rana came to understand a deeper truth, success comes through hard work, not from chasing shortcuts. Just like every tree that rises to the sky begins its journey from a tiny seed buried in darkness, so must a man rise with effort.

Rana focused on his land. He took care of his cattle, applied new technology in farming, raised better breeds of cows, and soon opened a small dairy. At first, he sold milk locally, prices were good. Each year, he grew. Soon, he had more cows than he could manage alone. He expanded from selling raw milk to producing yogurt, cheese, and milk-based drinks. Then came the factory. Then came exports. He started buying milk from nearby villages too. A second dairy was built, then a third. Before long, Rana had become one of the richest men in the area.

And yet, not a single rupee of his fortune had ever gone into Payja and Pa Shida's dream of making gold.

He used to sit and watch them fail, smiling to himself. Every time, it was something small a flicker in the fire, a missing grain of mineral, or some forgotten chemical and they'd say, "Just a little more. Next time it will work."

Rana tried to explain to them: "Success isn't hidden in shortcuts. It lies in walking the straight road with devotion and work." But the answer was always the same from Payja: "Once we make gold, we'll buy your business. Your cows. Your land."

And Rana would just laugh.

Rani, now a mother of five, had moved to a larger city. She had long given up trying to bring life into Payja's dead fish. She had settled for her husband's dullness but sometimes, just sometimes, she visited a shop in the city where someone invited her into the back room. Maybe the taste of shark still lingered on her tongue.

Payja had nothing left. No land, no business. He now worked in a factory just to stay alive. He asked Daniel for money, but Daniel refused. He knew any help would only fuel more experiments, more dreams that had no roots.

No one helped him anymore. But he still refused to change. In his heart, he remained the same man he was ten years ago, dreaming of the old canal, naked dips in summer, watermelon in hand, smoking hash under the sun with his friends. He was still waiting for that moment to return.

But time had walked on. No one had time for hashish or watermelons or naked swims in the canal. Everyone had their own families, their own lives. When life gives, it takes too. That's the truth.

Daniel had everything now a house, money, status, but not a single friend to swim naked with under the sun.

No more card games at Rana's house. No late-night laughter. They were never together again, one in the east, one in the north. One is busy growing wealth, the other busy fighting poverty.

Daniel's journey had reached its final chapter. He was in India, searching now for the last piece, the water of the 22 kunds. He flew from Delhi to Madurai, then took a bus.

Madurai was a small city, vibrant and full of life. The people of the South amazed him, soft-spoken, beautiful, and honest. He stayed for a few days, tasted the local food, flavors that exploded like fireworks and realized how wrong he'd been taught. In the North, people mocked the South, called it backward. But here, he found kindness, cleanliness, and education. Not once did someone cheat him. Unlike Delhi, where even a taxi driver would double the fare if they spotted a tourist.

He boarded an old AC bus to Rameshwaram.

He stood out. His face, his clothes, his vibe, everything about him said he didn't belong. And when the bus reached the Long Sea Bridge, the driver called him up front to enjoy the view.

Soon Daniel reached Rameshwaram. It was late at night. The air smelled of salt and incense, and a light breeze carried the sounds of temple bells from somewhere far. He needed rest before he could begin his final search.

He found a modest hotel near the temple complex. The rooms were simple, just a cot, a fan, and a jug of water but it was peaceful. Most of the guests were pilgrims, here for one purpose: to bathe in the sacred 22 kunds, and to touch the footsteps of Lord Ram.

In the great epic *Ramayana*, Lord Ram set out to rescue his wife, Sita, who had been taken by the demon king Ravan to Lanka, now Sri Lanka. When Ram and his army reached the shores of the southern sea, they had to find a way to cross the vast waters. It was here, in Rameshwaram, that Lord Ram prayed to Lord Shiva for strength, guidance, and victory.

As the story goes, Ram made a lingam out of sand and offered it with deep devotion to Shiva. Pleased with his devotion, Shiva blessed Ram and promised him success in battle. This sand lingam, over time, became the spiritual core of what we now call the Ramanathaswamy Temple.

Before building the bridge to Lanka, *Ram Setu*, or Adam's Bridge, Ram and his army bathed in the sacred ponds (kunds) near the seashore to purify themselves. These kunds were blessed by sages, rishis, and gods themselves. Each of the 22 kunds came to represent a unique spiritual quality, patience, clarity, forgiveness, truth, humility.

Over the centuries, these sacred water bodies have been preserved. The temple was built around them, and pilgrims from all over the world now come to bathe in each of the 22 kunds before offering prayers inside the sanctum.

The receptionist at the hotel looked up from his desk and asked Daniel, "Would you like to book a special pooja?"

"A special pooja?" Daniel raised his eyebrows. "What do you mean?"

"You can pay a fee, and a temple pundit will take you inside," the receptionist explained. "He'll guide you through all the rituals, and you won't have to wait in long queues."

"How much does it cost?" asked Daniel.

"There's a fixed temple fee five thousand rupees. As for the pundit, you can give whatever you wish."

"And what do people usually pay the pundit?"

"Some give five hundred, some a thousand. It's up to you."

Daniel thought it was a fair deal. It would save him time and give him deeper insight into the rituals. "Okay," he said. "Book it."

The next morning, long before sunrise, Daniel stood outside the temple gates at 4 a.m. The scene was breathtaking. The sky was still dark but already hundreds of devotees had gathered, dressed in white, murmuring prayers. The temple's silhouette rose like a memory of a forgotten age.

Daniel waited by the entrance, expecting a white-haired sage draped in a single piece of cloth, dhoti, Rud Raksha beads, ash on his forehead. But instead, a young man pulled up on a motorcycle.

"Let's go," the pundit said, hopping off the bike. Daniel followed, slightly amused.

The pundit was guiding another family too, an elderly couple and their daughter from Delhi. Daniel could sense something in their faces. A trace of worry lingered in the mother's eyes, and the father's silence said more than words.

The temple inside was stunning. The stone pillars were ancient and carved with intricate scenes, gods, battles, prayers, and devotion frozen in time. The pundit leaned toward Daniel and said, "This temple is over five thousand years old. This is the place where Ram himself worshipped Shiva before building the Ram Setu."

Then came the 22 kunds.

The first well stood like a silent guardian. The pundit filled a brass bucket and poured the cold water over Daniel's head. The shock of the water hit him hard. It felt like something sacred, pure, ancient, and alive. They moved quickly from one well to the next. Each had a name etched in stone. Each had a different feeling, some deeper, some warmer, some still as glass.

Daniel had come prepared. At each kund, he filled a bottle, carefully labeling them as he went. Water from all 22 kunds, this was part of the mission. It took nearly an hour, and by the time they finished, the sky had turned blue and golden, and the temple came alive in the morning light.

The final darshan came next. The pundit took them to the sanctum, where three Shiv lings stood one installed by Ram, another by Hanuman, and one by Sita. Daniel watched as lamps flickered and chants echoed. The priest performed the pooja with practiced grace, and each time, Daniel handed over a small offering as Dakshina.

Four hours passed. As they stepped outside into the sunlight, the pundit turned to Daniel and said, "It's done."

Daniel nodded. "How much should I pay you?"

"Five thousand five hundred for the pooja and temple fee. One thousand for the items used in rituals. And whatever you feel for Dakshina."

Daniel handed him seven thousand rupees. The pundit counted, looked up, and said, "This isn't enough. I spent four hours with you."

Daniel was stunned. The tone was unexpectedly demanding, transactional. This was supposed to be sacred work. But instead of arguing, he sighed and paid him more.

By now, the sun had risen fully. The streets were bustling. But Daniel's mission was complete.

He had everything now, the glowing herb from Kashmir, water from all 22 kunds in Rameshwaram, and the four poisons he had purchased from Delhi. These items held no personal meaning for him. But for his friends, for the ones who once believed in gold, who once sent Kala on this path they meant everything.

Daniel thought of Kala, whose journey ended in the shadows of Kashmir, and of Payja and Pa Shida, still chasing alchemy. He had done this for them. Not for gold. Not for glory. But for friendship. For memory of Kala.

Daniel stepped out of the temple into the burning daylight. The pooja took hours. His body still carried the chill of the kunds, but his spirit felt light. He walked towards the shore where the sea met the land like a lover's embrace. The wind was salty and sacred.

People bathed in the holy water, some sat silently with folded hands, some prayed, others simply let the waves kiss their feet. There was peace on every face, a kind of still joy that comes when you feel the presence of something greater.

Further down the shore, Daniel noticed a crowd gathered near a tree. He walked closer, curious. In the center of the circle sat a man half in shadow, half in light. A saint. Naked, covered in white ash, beard long and flowing like a river of snow. He was in deep meditation, unmoved by the voices and footsteps around him. Devotees came one by one to touch his feet with reverence, whispering prayers of hope or pain.

Daniel joined them. He bowed low and placed his hand on the saint's feet and suddenly, time stopped.

His breath hitched.

His eyes widened.

The body was ash-covered, the hair different, even the face bore the years like forgotten poems but what caught Daniel by surprise was something no disguise could ever change.

He had seen that penis before.

More precisely, he had stood beside that same penis at the canal back in their village, laughing, bathing, watermelon in hand, smoking hashish with friends.

It was him. **Kala.**

Tears rolled down Daniel's face before he could even whisper the name. "Kalay…" he said, voice trembling.

But the saint didn't move.

Daniel sat down beside him. His heartbeat like a drum inside a temple. He didn't know if he should speak again or just wait. So, he waited.

Minutes passed.

And finally, Kala opened his eyes.

Daniel was sitting in front of him, staring into his soul.

"What can I do for you, Bhakta?" said Kala in a calm, godlike voice.

Daniel leaned forward, his eyes pleading. "Please talk to me… Kalay," he whispered.

The moment the voice touched Kala's ears; he froze.

He didn't see faces anymore, he only saw Mahadev in every soul. But the voice, that voice, pierced through the smoke of his visions.

It was Daniel.

A flicker of emotion crossed his face. His lips trembled into the ghost of a smile.

"At last," he said softly. "At last, you are here. I knew… only you could find me. Only you could walk this far. Only you could reach where I am now."

"Why didn't you go back? Why didn't you send them what you came for? Why are you here?" a storm of questions burst out of Daniel's mouth all at once.

"Calm down, calm down," Kala said gently, his voice as steady as the ocean behind him. "You will know everything… just wait and see."

He turned to a man nearby and whispered something. Within minutes, food was brought for both. Daniel didn't take his eyes off Kala for a moment. He was watching him with awe and disbelief. This was the same man who once jumped across a border in madness, who had risked his life for a dream, who had vanished without a trace. And now he was here, an Aghori. A saint. A mystery wrapped in ash and silence.

Kala looked up and said, "Daniel, life isn't what we thought it was back in the village. It's something else altogether. And you've realized that too, haven't you?"

"Yes," Daniel replied softly. "I've seen it with my own eyes."

"But then… answer me this," Daniel continued, unable to hold it in. "Why didn't you send the poisons, the herbs, the water to Payja? You were supposed to complete the mission."

"Have you found everything now?" Kala asked.

"Yes, I have."

"Are you happy?"

"No… I never wanted these things for myself. I did it for Payja. I came to India to find your grave," Daniel said, staring into the sand.

"I know," Kala replied, a faint smile on his face. "And today… you've found it."

Daniel looked up in surprise.

"My grave?" he asked.

Kala nodded slowly. "Yes. You found my grave. I died long ago, Daniel. The Kala you knew… he's gone."

"But you still didn't answer my question," Daniel said again. "Why didn't you send those things? Why didn't you help Payja make the gold?"

Kala placed his hand on Daniel's shoulder. His voice was soft, steady, almost like a prayer.

"You know, Daniel, the story we heard about that saint who turned copper into gold, we misunderstood it. It wasn't the herbs or the poisons or the waters of the 22 kunds that turned into metal. It was his struggle… his devotion… his transformation. We remembered the recipe but forgot the journey. We remembered the magic but ignored the meditation. That saint… he traveled from the Himalayas to the southern tip of this land, the very place where you sit now. He didn't turn copper into gold. He turned himself into someone who could turn anything into anything."

Daniel sat in silence. The words hung in the air like sacred smoke.

"You mean…?"

"Yes," Kala whispered. "You understood it."

Daniel nodded, quietly. "But still… send these things to Payja. At least he won't think I betrayed him. Let him believe I did my part."

Kala smiled. "Yes, you're right."

And so, Daniel went to the nearest post office. He packed the herbs, the poisons, the water from 22 kunds, all of it. With it, he wrote a note:

"This is what you desired. Nothing is missing now. Go ahead, try your luck. But my belief still stands that you won't succeed. You can't change the laws of nature."

Then he returned for one final meeting with Kala.

"I should go back to Sweden now," Daniel said.

Kala was calm. He had been joyful throughout their time together. There was a stillness in him, like a man who had finally become part of the wind, the trees, and the sky.

"Why didn't you go back to your family?" Daniel asked.

"Because I don't think anyone needed me anymore. My relations had already buried me in their hearts. Life had moved on. I couldn't go back there to die again."

Daniel sat still. His chest was heavy with everything he had heard.

Kala told him everything, his story, his journey, the transformations, the meditations, the truths he had seen. Daniel cried.

"Please," Kala said softly, "never tell anyone what you saw here. No one should know I'm alive."

"I won't," Daniel promised.

"And tell me, is there anything you want from me?"

Daniel looked at him with tears. "Yes… I want to see what you see."

Kala looked deeply into his eyes.

"Okay," he said at last. "But remember, once you see it… there is no going back."

If your God will open your eyes you will see Him in each and every creation.

Daniel nodded.

Kala reached into his small bag and pulled out some ash.

"Take off your clothes," he said.

Daniel did so without question.

"Close your eyes."

Daniel closed them.

Kala rubbed the ash gently over Daniel's bare skin, murmuring a prayer so soft that it sounded like the wind.

"Now," he whispered, "open your eyes."

Daniel opened his eyes.

And suddenly his lips trembled.

He gasped. "Jesus… Jesus… Jesus…"

Tears rolled down his cheeks.

Everywhere, he saw Jesus.